DARK HARVEST

Norman Partridge

A Tom Doherty Associates Book.

New York

DARK HARVEST

Copyright © 2006 by Norman Partridge

Originally published in 2006 by Cemetery Dance Publications

A Tor Book
Published by Tom Doherty Associates, LLC
175 Fifth Avenue
New York, NY 10010

www.tor.com

Tor® is a registered trademark of Tom Doherty Associates, LLC.

Library of Congress Cataloging-in-Publication Data

Partridge, Norman.
    Dark harvest / Norman Partridge. — 1st Tor ed.
        p. cm.
    "A Tom Doherty Associates Book."
    ISBN-13: 978-0-7653-1911-1
    ISBN-10: 0-7653-1911-X
    1. Teenagers—Fiction. 2. Middle West—Fiction. 3. Coming of age—Fiction. I. Title.

PS3566.A77236D37 2007
813'.54—dc22

                                                                    2007019650

First Tor Edition: September 2007

Printed in the United States of America

10   9   8

For Ed Gorman

PART ONE
Stories

A Midwestern town. You know its name. You were born there.

It's Halloween, 1963 . . . and getting on toward dark. Things are the same as they've always been. There's the main street, the old brick church in the town square, the movie theater—this year with a Vincent Price double-bill. And past all that is the road that leads out of town. It's black as a licorice whip under an October sky, black as the night that's coming and the long winter nights that will follow, black as the little town it leaves behind.

The road grows narrow as it hits the outskirts. It does not meander. Like a planned path of escape, it cleaves a sea of quarter sections planted thick with summer corn.

But it's not summer anymore. Like I said, it's Halloween.

All that corn has been picked, shucked, eaten.

All those stalks are dead, withered, dried.

In most places, those stalks would have been plowed under long ago. That's not the way it works around here. You remember. Corn's harvested by hand in these parts. Boys who live in this town spend their summers doing the job under a blazing sun that barely bothers to go down. And once those boys are tanned straight through and that crop's picked, those cornstalks die rooted in the ground. They're not plowed under until the first day of November. Until then the silent rows are home to things that don't mind living among the dead. Rats, snakes, frogs . . . creatures that will take flight before the first light of the coming morning or die beneath a circular blade that scores both earth and flesh without discrimination.

Yeah. That's the way it works around here. There are things living in these fields tonight that will, by rights, be dead by tomorrow morning. One of them hangs on a splintery pole, its roots burrowing deep in rich black soil. Green vines climb through tattered clothes nailed to the pole and its crosspiece. They twist through the legs of worn jeans like tendons, twine like a cripple's spine through a tattered denim jacket. Rounded leaves take succor from those vines like organs fed by blood vessels, and from the hearts of those leaves green tendrils sprout, and the leaves and the vines and the tendrils fill up that coat and the arms that come with it.

A thicker vine creeps through the neck of that jacket, following the last few inches of splintery pole like a backbone, widening into a rough stem that roots in the thing balanced on the pole's flat crown.

That thing is heavy, and orange, and ripe.

That thing is a pumpkin.

The afternoon sun lingers on the pumpkin's face, and then the afternoon sun is gone. Quiet hangs in the cornfield. No breeze rustles the dead stalks; no wind rustles the tattered clothes of the thing hanging from the pole. The licorice-whip road is empty, silent, still. No cars coming into town, no cars leaving.

It's that way for a long time. Then darkness falls.

A car comes. A door slams. Footsteps in the cornfield—the sound of a man shouldering through brittle stalks. The butcher knife that fills his hand gleams beneath the rising moon, and then the blade goes black as the man bends low.

Twisted vines and young creepers root at the base of the pole. The man's sharp blade severs all. Next he goes to work with a claw hammer. Rusty nails grunt loose from old wood. A tattered leg slips free . . . then another . . . and then a tattered arm. . . .

The thing they call the October Boy drops to the ground.

But you already know about him. After all, you grew up here. There aren't any secrets left for you. You know the story as well as I do.

Pete McCormick knows the story, too . . . part of it, anyway. Pete just turned sixteen. He's been in town his whole life, but he's never managed to fit in. And the last year's been especially tough. His mom died of cancer last winter, and his dad drank away his job at the grain elevator the following spring. There's enough rotten luck in that little sentence to bust anyone's chops.

So it's not like the walls have never closed in on Pete around here, but just lately they've been jamming his shoulders like he's caught in a drill press. He gets in trouble a couple times and gets picked up by the cops—good old Officer Ricks in his shiny black-and-white Dodge. First time around, it's a lecture. Second time, it's a nightstick to the kidneys. Pete comes home all bruised up and pisses blood for a couple of days. He waits for his old man to slam him back in line the way he would have before their whole world hit a wall, maybe take a hunk out of that bastard Ricks while he's at it. But his father doesn't even say a word, so Pete figures, *Well, it looks like you're finally on your own, Charlie Brown, and what are you going to do about that?*

For Pete, it's your basic wake-up call. Once and for all he decides he doesn't much care for his Podunk hometown. Doesn't like all that corn. Doesn't like all that quiet. Sure as hell doesn't like Officer Ricks.

And maybe he's not so crazy about his father, either. Summer rolls around and the old man starts hitting the bottle pretty steady. Could be he's noticed the changes in his son, because he starts telling stories—all of a sudden he's really

big with the stories. *We'll get back on our feet soon, Pete.
They'll call me back to work at the elevator, because that
chucklehead Kirby will screw everything up.* That gets to be
one of Pete's favorites. Right up there with: *I'm going to quit
the drinking, son. For you and your sister. I promise I'll quit
it soon.*

It's like the old man has a fish on the line, and he's
trying to reel it in with words. But Pete gets tired of
listening. He's smart enough to know that words don't
matter unless they're walking the hard road that leads to the
truth. And, sure, he can understand what's going on. Sure,
the nightstick that life put to his old man makes the solid
hunk of oak Officer Ricks used to bust up Pete look like a
toothpick. But understanding all that doesn't make listening
to his old man's pipe dreams any easier.

And that's what his father's words turn out to be. The
bossman down at the elevator never calls, and the old man's
drinking doesn't stop, and things don't get any better for them.
Things just keep on getting worse. As the summer wanes, Pete
often catches himself daydreaming about the licorice-whip
road that leads out of town. He wonders what it would be
like out there somewhere else . . . far away from here . . . on
his own. And pretty soon that road finds its way into another
story making the rounds, because—hey—it's September
now, and it's about time folks started in on that one crazy yarn
everyone around here spins at that time of year.

Pete catches bits of it around town. First from a couple
of football players waiting to get their flat-tops squared

at the barber shop, later from a bunch of guys standing in line at the movie theater one hot Saturday night. And pretty soon the story picks up steam at the high school, too. Again, Pete only hears snatches of it—in the bathroom out back of the auto shop where guys go to sneak cigarettes, in detention hall after school—and, sure, it's pretty crazy stuff, but the craziest thing is that those snatches of conversation all fall within the same parameters, and that simple fact is enough to start Pete thinking this might be the rare kind of story that actually makes the trip from the campfire to the cold hard street.

"Got me a bat. Brand new Louisville Slugger."

"That ain't what you need. It's too hard to swing a bat when you're on the run, and you're too slow as it is, anyway. Just look at that table muscle hanging over your belt. You couldn't catch my great-great grandma rolling her ass uphill in a wheelchair with a couple of blown tires if your life depended on it."

"I don't have to catch your great-great grandma, stupid. I don't have to catch anyone. *All I have to do is plant myself in the right place. I'll let my chuckleheaded cousins do the catching. They'll flush that sucker like a prize buck, corral him in a blind alley. And that's where I'll be waiting, all ready to take my cuts."*

"Fat chance. You spend the night of the Run hanging out in some stupid alley, you might as well set up housekeeping there for a whole goddamn year."

"Uh-uh. You boys'll be the ones who end up hanging around this jerkwater town for another year, not me. I'll have a walking nightmare's carcass chained to my bumper, and I'll be across the Line and gone for good by the time you take your first piss of the morning."

Pete's been thinking about that conversation for the last few days, putting it together with all the other stories he's heard. Adding it up one way, then adding it up another just to see if he can make it come out any other way than the crazy spookshow equation it wears for a face.

And, hey, just lately Pete's had plenty of time to think about all that stuff. Because it's the tail end of October now, and his father's had him locked in his bedroom for the last five days. Nothing to eat in there. Only water to drink, and—when the old man's feeling generous—maybe a glass of OJ that's a long way from fresh-squeezed. You want sufficient opportunity to become a believer, well, there you go. Try feeding a five-day hunger with some OJ that tastes like a cup of freezer burn, and nothing to wash it down but a bunch of words you can't get out of your head.

But even with all that chewing around inside him, Pete can't quite buy into the stories he's been hearing. Oh, sure, he can believe the part about the kids and the crazy stuff they get up to with their baseball bats and pitchforks on Halloween night. After his run-in with Officer Ricks, he's certain his hayseed hometown could breed a nasty little square dance like that. But the other part—the spookshow part—Pete's not so sure he can make the whole trip there.

You can't really blame him, can you? I mean, think about it. Remember when you were just a little kid, the first time you noticed your older brother locked up tight for five days and nights during the last week of October? Remember the first time you heard that the whole deal had something to do with a pumpkin-headed scarecrow that runs around on Halloween night? It wasn't exactly easy to believe that one no matter how scared you were, was it?

Not until you experienced it yourself, of course.

Until you were the guy locked up in your bedroom.

Until you were the guy who saw what went down when you hit the streets on Halloween night.

But Pete hasn't seen any of that. Not yet. Like I said, he just turned sixteen. Tonight is his first crack at the Run. So it's not really surprising that his *disbelief* isn't completely *suspended*. But he's getting there. And the more Pete thinks about it, the less important the whole spookshow equation seems. The way Pete sees it, what he believes or disbelieves doesn't really matter much when you look at the big picture.

Do that, and other stuff starts to matter.

Uh-huh. What matters is that his old man has kept him locked up for five days. What matters is that he hasn't had anything to eat. What matters is that he's dead cold certain it's been just that way for every other guy in town between the ages of sixteen and nineteen. The high school is closed—has been for five days. The streets are empty. And guys all over town are pacing crackerbox bedrooms in the wee small hours, gearing up for Halloween night like bulls penned up in tight little chutes.

Pete sits on his bed and thinks about that. Right about now, it seems like a pretty full bucket of *validation*. So he lets his mind tote that sucker, and he gets comfortable with the load.

He thinks about baseball bats and pitchforks, and butcher knives, and two-by-fours studded with nails, and a couple hundred young guys hitting the streets as darkness falls.

He thinks about a scarecrow running around with a pumpkin for a head.

He thinks about what running down that scarecrow might mean for a guy like him.

Then, as the old Waltham clock on his nightstand ticks down the dying embers of Halloween evening, he stops thinking about all that stuff.

After that, he only thinks about a couple of things, the really important things.

He thinks about the door to his bedroom swinging open.

He thinks about what he'll do when he steps outside.

If the October Boy had knees he'd be on them, kneeling as he is at the shrine of the autumn moon.

Or maybe it's the shrine of the man with the knife. After all, that's who's looming over the October Boy like an onyx statue, his silhouette standing between the Boy and the large dome of a moon half-risen against the indigo sky.

For a moment, the Boy is lost in the man's shadow. He tilts his blind, blank face upward. Then the man kneels, and moonlight washes both of them. The butcher knife catches the light like a mirror as he raises it. His other hand closes over the pumpkin stem, and he holds the Boy's head steady, and he sets about his work.

Determined strokes of the blade give the Boy a face. First come the eyes, a pair of triangles sliced narrow. Then the nose, which, of course, is wider—a barbed arrowhead of a hole that will provide the illusion of flared nostrils when finished.

The blade works steadily as the nose takes shape. The pumpkin's skin is thick, the meat beneath thicker. The carver flicks severed chunks to the dirt below. His wrist begins to ache, but his hand does not hesitate until an exhalation exits the October Boy's spiked nostrils, warming the man's cold fingers.

The butcher knife freezes in mid-air. The man's own breath is quite suddenly trapped in his chest. He holds the stem tightly, and he stares at the half-face in front of him, knowing that he has made it what it is and that he will make it what it will be. As if reading his mind, the October Boy's narrow eyes grow narrower still. He draws a shallow breath through his barbed nose, and a dull flickering light blooms behind those empty triangular sockets.

This unsettles the man, for there is no candle within the Boy's hollow head. Still, the light is there, and so is the wet crackle of flame tasting fibrous yellow strands. These things the man recognizes clearly, though he cannot explain them.

So best not to think about it, the man tells himself.

No point in thinking, because there's no explaining any of it.

Tonight, everything's just the way it is.

Tonight, everything's chiseled in stone.

Yes. The man with the knife could not possibly see this night any other way. For a long moment, he stares into the pair of flickering sockets where the Boy's eyes should be. The man does not blink; the October Boy can't. The Boy draws another tentative breath, and his exhalation carries the rich scents of scorched cinnamon and gunpowder and melting wax. Somehow, the mingled smells steady the man, and he raises the knife once more and sets about finishing the work he has begun.

Twin rows of jagged teeth appear below the arrowhead gap of the nose. Yellow light flickers across the man's hand as the Boy inhales through his spiked mouth. His breaths are still shallow, still weak. But the light from his eyes paints harsh triangles on the man's face as he carves, and the man works faster now, cutting twin ends into a wicked smile that cleaves cheekbones and just misses stabbing the October Boy's eyes.

The man's knife hand drops to his side; his other hand releases the stem attached to the pumpkin's crown. The Boy's head bobs low—by rights it should fall off his shoulders, for in truth he has no neck to support it. But this changes quickly as green creepers climb the twisted vine, which leads to the stem, twining as they go, growing thicker and darker as they angle toward the base of the pumpkin. They raise the Boy's head on a strong, braided neck that drives barbed tendrils into the gourd itself.

That corded neck turns from green to brown as it roots in the heavy globe. Fresh growth scabs over with dark, rough bark. Vines and leaves rustle within the Boy's coat as he takes his first deep breath. The Boy raises his head as the cool evening air fills him. He holds that breath for a long moment, and then it leaves him in a spiced exhalation.

A feeble tongue of flame follows it . . . and what most certainly is a word.

But the man with the knife will not acknowledge a word from the thing that stands before him. He has not come to listen to words. No. He has come to do a job that must be done, and that is what he will do. No more, no less. So he turns away with the knife still in his hands, and he walks to the road. The October Boy's scrabbled footfalls follow the man's even steps as he crosses the cornfield. But the man does not turn around, and it is only when he hears the rhythm of his own boot heels on hard pavement that his mind returns to the next task this night requires.

The man's car is barely a year old. It's black and sleek—not at all like the other cars you see around here. He sets the butcher knife on the hood and opens the door. There's a grocery bag on the front seat, waiting there on expensive upholstery. The bag is heavy with candy. The man grabs a couple Big Hunks and stuffs them into one of the Boy's coat pockets. He digs deep in the grocery bag and fills the other pocket with Clark bars. Next he unfastens the front button of the October Boy's coat, and he shoves candy through those ropes of vines. Oh Henry!s; Hershey's bars; Abba-Zaba's.

Handfuls of Candy Corn nestle between leaves like secrets wedged into green envelopes. Red Vines and Bit-O-Honeys fill the gaps. The October Boy staggers a bit, for the man's hand is as cold as the coming night, and the load is heavier than one might think.

And so he totters, but he will not fall. The Boy is not made that way. His severed-root feet scrape as he backpedals a few steps across the black road, and he leans against the car for support. The man closes on him and shoves one last fistful of candy against the gnarled vine of his backbone, and the Boy's sawtoothed smile becomes a grimace. Perhaps another word waits within, in his mouth, ready to travel another tongue of flame. But before either thing can leave him, the man who has given him a face fills the Boy's sliced grin with a handful of Atomic Fireballs, and then another, and another.

The light grows dimmer in the October Boy's mouth.

The light grows brighter behind his eyes.

Soon the grocery bag is empty. The man balls it up and tosses it into the field. Now there is only one thing left to do. He retrieves the knife from the hood of the car. It only takes a second to do this, but in that second the man stares at the dead field and the indigo blanket of sky that has now grown very dark, and he sees the cold stars glimmering above him and the bright empty dome of the rising moon, and as he turns his gaze travels from the things that hang in the sky to the ribbon of asphalt that waits at his feet—the black road that carves a midnight path toward the cold white glow marking the town.

The man stares at the October Boy. He does not say a word. His actions speak for him. He extends the butcher knife. Thick tendril fingers vine around the hilt as the Boy takes it. And now the man's hand is empty, and his white fingers stiffen as they stretch through the darkness, tracing the path of the road.

Every finger but one curls into a fist.

The man points toward the town.

The Boy with the knife starts toward it.

Pete hears them in the street. He turns out the bedroom light and parts the threadbare drapes so he can see what's going on out there. Yeah. It's just like everyone said. The town's teenage male population is on the move. They're running in packs, like dogs turned loose for the hunt.

The old oak in Pete's front yard chokes off the moonlight, but he recognizes three guys from his gym class as they pass beneath the dull glow cast by the streetlight on the corner. They're loping down the middle of the street, hooting at shadows as if calling down a dare. One of them has a baseball bat, another a ball-peen hammer, the last a two-by-four bristling with nails—

A car horn blares behind them as a rust-pocked heap runs a stop sign and makes the corner. The boys scatter, and the gap between two of them is just wide enough to accommodate a beat-up Chrysler hardtop with a pair of headlights that blaze like a Gorgon's eyeballs. At least that's the way those headlights seem to Pete, and he freezes behind his bedroom window as the twin beams hit the glass.

For a brief moment, the headlights frame him like a portrait nailed to a wall. The Chrysler completes its turn and roars up the street. Just that fast it's gone, and Pete's standing there all alone in the darkness. Outside, two of the guys from his gym class peel their skinny asses off the asphalt and dust themselves off while their buddy needles them from Pete's front yard. "Crenshaw and his rattletrap," the guy laughs. "Your sweet little asses nearly got chopped, girls. You almost greased that shitheap's gearbox but good."

The guy goes on like that for a while. He's got a mouth on him, all right. His chatter seems pretty funny, considering, and Pete almost laughs until the other guys bark down the Mouth with a few choice insults of their own.

Those guys pick up the things they dropped when they scattered—that ball-peen hammer, and that two-by-four studded with nails. And then there's nothing left to laugh about. Suddenly, it's like that car was never there at all. The two kids take a few cuts at the shadows and move on, and their friend the Mouth silently cocks his baseball bat over his shoulder and follows them PDQ, as if the last thing he wants in the world is to be left alone.

Seeing the last kid do that, Pete feels a hole open up inside him. Not that he needed anyone to paint him a picture, but that little incident just did the job, because there's no way he can ignore the score when it comes to this game. Pete's alone right now, locked up in his room, and he's going to be alone when he hits the streets. No friends, no car, no backup. And that's not a feeling with a whole lot of *good* in it, even if you're used to going solo. Fact is, Pete's pretty sure that he'd be hiding under his bed right now if he had any sense at all.

But Pete knows he'd never turn chicken like that. Not as long as he has a reason to stand on his own two feet. He might not be able to put a name to that reason, but he knows he's got it. It's somewhere down deep inside him, in a quiet place his father could never understand . . . or maybe it's somewhere just down the hall, behind another bedroom door marked with a little girl's handprint in pink paint. And just as he's thinking that, his bedroom door swings open. A hard slab of light fills the space, and a dull yellow carpet stitched by a single Westinghouse bulb stretches from the doorway to his bed.

His old man stands there in the hallway. Pete can't see him clearly with the exposed bulb dangling behind his father's head, but he can see enough. The old man's hardly weaving at all, but Pete knows that he's drunk. And when his father follows his shadow into the room, Pete notices that the old man's got something in his hand.

Pete can't see what it is yet. Neither can he see his father's face. And then the old man turns on the bedroom light, and right off Pete sees everything real clearly. All the broken things that lie buried behind the old man's eyes, and the honed thing gripped in his fist.

The old man hands the machete to his son.

"This saw me through the Run when I was your age. I figure it'll do the same for you tonight."

Pete runs his thumb over the oiled blade. Maybe he should keep his mouth shut. Maybe. But after five days locked up in this shoebox of a room, he just can't do it.

"Looks like this thing could do some damage if a guy had the guts to put it to work."

Pete speaks those words evenly. His tone is matter-of-fact. But those words are bait tossed in the water, and Pete knows it, and so does his old man.

"You have something to say to me, son?"

"I just did."

"Listen, I know what you're thinking—"

"No you don't, so don't pretend that you do."

"Pete, I know how you feel. But it's one night, and you'll get through it. And tomorrow I'll get to work on things. I mean it. I'll call Joe Grant down at the elevator, and maybe I can patch things up and get my job back—"

"It's too late for that, Dad. I'm tired of listening to you tell me how things are going to change when I know they won't. You lost your chance to do that when you crawled inside a bottle."

"Wait a second, boy. Hear me out—"

"No. Our backs are to the wall. There's only one way out, so I'm going to take it. I'm going out there tonight, and I'm going to change things. I'm gonna win the Run, and I'm not gonna do it with words."

His old man grabs Pete then. It's exactly the wrong thing to do. Pete pushes his father away, harder than he should, and he snatches his frayed denim jacket off the bed, and he heads for the doorway.

Outside, some guy screams in the street, but Pete doesn't jump. Up the block, an axe handle rattles across a gap-toothed picket fence, but Pete doesn't twitch. He starts down the hallway, leaving his bedroom behind without a backward glance.

The old man's calling after him. Pete hears the words, but they don't matter now that he's said his piece. So he buries those words under his footsteps, and he leaves them behind. He only cares about what's up ahead, ready to charge his ass like a rusty Chrysler with a pair of Gorgon headlights. And he walks down the shitty little hallway with its lone lightbulb and nicotine-stained paint, and he passes his kid sister's bedroom, but not fast enough to escape the muffled sobs behind the eight-year-old's painted handprint on the door. Kim shouts his name as another pack of guys scream by in the street, but Pete doesn't slow a step.

He can't afford to. That thing up ahead is suddenly real, and it's pulling at him. *The October Boy.* It's all he's heard about for the last two months. The story's been drilled into him and spackled over. He knows what it is, and what it means.

If Pete's got the guts, he can grab it.

If he's got the smarts, it's all his.

So his lips stay buttoned as he opens the front door. His father's footsteps are dogging him now, and his little sister's still calling his name in a voice that's burning a hole straight through his heart, but he's through that door in a second, and he hits the street with his father's machete clutched tightly in his hand.

He runs into the night. His Chuck Taylors don't make a sound. But somehow, no matter how fast he humps it, that beat-up look in his father's eyes keeps the pace. Pete can outrun his father's words, but he can't outrun that look. It's welded to his spine like a shiny key stuck in the back of some cheap Japanese toy, and with every *click-clack* twist it winds his bones and muscles tighter, so when that key spins free he runs like the devil himself is cranking his gears.

And that's the way it is for our buddy Pete, all the way from his front door to the alley behind a rundown bungalow that faces North Harvest Street.

Pete's tennis shoes skid over gravel as he comes to a stop by the back fence. He cools his jets for a second, takes a quick look up the alley. There's no one else around. So he tosses the machete over the fence, then jumps the sucker himself.

He comes down on a weed-choked lawn that died about two months ago. The backyard's as empty as the alley. There's not even a dog, but that's no surprise. Because this house belongs to a cop named Jerry Ricks, and a brutal son of a bitch like Ricks sure wouldn't figure he'd need a dog to scare anyone in this town.

But Pete isn't scared. He's sure Ricks won't be anywhere close to home tonight—not with the Run kicking into gear. He also knows that the cop lives alone. So the house is dark. No lights on outside or in. Pete picks up the machete and crosses the lawn, dead grass crunching underfoot. There's a hose by the back stairs, and he turns it on and has a quick drink. The water tastes like rubber, but at least it's cold.

Pete sits down on the back steps and catches his breath. There's an overhang covering a cracked cement patio, but it doesn't look like the kind of place anyone would pick for a summertime cookout or anything. Hanging from one thick beam in the center of the overhang is a heavy bag—the kind boxers use. For a second Pete remembers the job Ricks did on him with that nightstick. For another second he pictures the cop out here, working on that bag, pummeling hard-packed canvas with his fists the same way he jammed Pete's kidneys with that nightstick, grinning like an ape while he works up a real good sweat.

That's enough to get Pete moving again. He tries the back door, but even Jerry Ricks doesn't trust his reputation that far—the door is locked. So Pete goes around to the side of the house, finds a window set low enough in the wall that he can work on without hunting for a ladder.

It's a double-hung job—the easiest kind. Pete works the machete blade between the stool and the bottom rail, levering the steel sharply. This time luck's on his side. The lower sash rises, which means the window wasn't even locked.

Pete reaches inside and drops the machete to the floor. He slips over the sill and closes the window behind him. It's dark inside the house, but he doesn't turn on a light. Instead he waits for his eyes to adjust, and it doesn't take long.

There's the machete, lying on the floor. Pete snatches it up. If things go the way he's planned, he won't need it much longer. The way Pete's got things figured, a twenty-year-old machete isn't going to cut it when it comes to the job that needs doing tonight. It might have been good enough for his father all those years ago, but Pete's all through fooling himself about what kind of guy his dad is. What did the machete get his old man, anyway? Twenty years stuck in this town. Twenty years spinning his wheels, so he could crawl inside a bottle when things got tough.

No way Pete's going to end up like that. That's why he's here, taking a chance no other kid has even contemplated. Any other night, breaking into a house owned by the town's leading hard-ass would earn you a one-way ticket to the graveyard. But not tonight. If Pete gets out of here without getting caught, and if things go the way he plans out there on the streets, well, no one will care how many laws he broke in this stinking little crackerbox as long as he ends up grabbing the brass ring before the bell in the old church steeple tolls midnight.

That's a whole lot of *ifs* to swallow, but there's no other way Pete can see this night going. Either he'll end up a winner, or he'll end up dead. As far as he's concerned, it's a *one way or the other* proposition. Forget settling. Forget compromise. Tonight he left all that behind in his father's house, and—

Hell, Pete doesn't have time to stand here jerking himself off with words. That's his father's game. *First things first* is the way he sees it. That means he's going to worry about his belly instead of his brain, because he's got a five-day hunger to kill if he wants to run full-out tonight.

He steps around the counter separating the dining room from the kitchen. Man, it's rank in there. A garbage can's jammed in the corner by the back door. A couple of empty TV-dinner trays that have done double-duty as ashtrays stick up over the rim, and shoved to one side is a nest of hamburger wrappers occupied by greasy fries that look like they're ready to start crawling.

The sight doesn't exactly whet the appetite, but Pete's so hungry it doesn't much matter. He sets the machete on the sidebar, opens the fridge, and takes a quick inventory. There's a carton of eggs, a jar of pickles, and a couple of apples that are on the far side of withered.

"Oh, man," he whispers, but he keeps looking. A couple of sixes of Burgie, bottles of mustard and mayo and ketchup, and—here comes the clincher—a quart bottle of orange juice.

That's it.

"Just my goddamn luck," Pete whispers, because OJ's the only thing he's had in the last five days. Still, he grabs the bottle and twists off the top, taking a long swallow as he steps over to the cupboards above the sink. Gotta be something better in there. Pete opens the door, but all he sees is a box of oatmeal, some pancake mix, and—

Behind him, the doorbell rings.

Pete freezes. Standing right there in Jerry Ricks's kitchen, with a bottle of OJ in his hand. He glances over the counter. He's got a straight view from the kitchen, through the dining room, to the attached living room. The drapes are wide open in there, and the front window is only a couple of feet from the door. All the doorbell ringer has to do is take a couple steps to the left and they'll be sure to spot Pete standing in front of the moonlit kitchen window.

So Pete moves quickly, trading the OJ for the machete as he steps into the dining room. The hallway that leads to the other side of the house lies just beyond. At least he'll be out of sight if he heads down there. . . .

The doorbell rings a second time. A floorboard creaks underfoot. Pete pauses. There's a little smoked-glass window set at head level in the front door—the kind of glass you can't see through clearly, but Pete can see well enough to tell that there's a shadow on it. By the height, his guess is that the shadow belongs to a man . . . maybe a friend of Ricks's . . . maybe another cop—

And Pete knows what the guy's thinking, because there are only so many things you can think when you're standing on the other side of someone's door. Either the guy will leave in another second or two, or maybe—just maybe—he might try the doorknob to see if the door is unlocked.

Just when Pete's sure that's going to happen, the shadow disappears from the dimpled glass. Footsteps click against the concrete steps leading down to the walk. In a second Pete's over at the living room window, just in time to spot a dark figure walking around to the driver's side of a sleek black Cadillac parked at the curb.

The man climbs inside and starts the engine. The car pulls away. Pete hurries down the hall. Forget food. Even if Jerry Ricks had something worth eating, Pete couldn't put anything in his stomach right now. He needs to find the thing he came for and get the hell out of here.

The first room Pete enters stinks just as bad as the kitchen. It's Ricks's bedroom. Cigarette butts are heaped in an ashtray by the bed. Dirty clothes lie on the floor, along with a couple of unfurled bandages that look like they were shed by a mummy—boxer's hand wraps.

No sheets or blankets, just a tangled sleeping bag and a pillow without a pillowcase on the mattress. There's a dresser on one wall, a nightstand in the corner. A bunch of junk in the dresser, and the only thing in the nightstand is a big stack of *Playboys*. That's not what Pete's looking for, either, so he tries the closet. On one side, several police uniforms hang in dry-cleaner bags. On the other side, there's a brand new vacuum cleaner, still in the box, with dust all over the top of it.

Jesus. Pete turns his back on Ricks's disaster area of a bedroom. There's another room at the end of the hall. That's gotta be the place he's looking for. He starts toward it, and he notices for the first time that the hallway walls are empty . . . so were the bedroom walls . . . so were the walls in the living room.

Every wall in this house is empty. There aren't any pictures here at all.

But Pete doesn't have time to wonder about that. He's thinking about the room at the end of the hall instead. The door is closed . . . locked. Now he's really rattled. Because he's thinking about that guy in the black Cadillac, wondering if he might come back. And he's wondering if maybe the guy was supposed to meet Ricks here, thinking that maybe Ricks might be a little late, maybe the lawman himself might be coming back any minute now—

Pete hauls back and kicks the door just below the knob. The molding splinters and the door flies open, banging against the wall with a thunderclap Pete's certain they'll hear at the police station a mile away.

No pictures in this room, either. Just a desk that looks like somebody's castoff . . . a chair with torn upholstery that looks the same . . . another heaped ashtray . . . and over there, in the corner, the thing that Pete came looking for.

A locked cabinet.

Yeah. The cabinet's the one piece of furniture in Jerry Ricks's house that looks like it cost some money. It's blond pine, polished to a heavy sheen, with a couple of grizzly bears painted on the locked doors. Those bears are reared up on their hind legs, teeth bared, claws slashing through forest green.

The grizzlies stop Pete cold, just for a second. He's not sure exactly why. Because now he's absolutely sure that the thing he needs is penned up in that cabinet, the same way he'd been penned up in his goddamn bedroom for five days and nights.

That thing is quiet.

It doesn't say a word.

But it can talk, all right.

It can talk in a way nothing alive can ignore.

Pete clenches his teeth and works fast. The machete flashes out, scoring polished wood. Pine slivers fly through the air like needles. A door panel shatters, and Pete tears it loose. A couple seconds later, the lock and its hasp clatter to the hardwood floor, and he's inside the cabinet.

A couple minutes after that, Pete backtracks through the kitchen, through the back door, across that dead lawn....

His father's machete is buried in one of Jerry Ricks's empty walls.

A stolen .45 semiautomatic is gripped in Pete McCormick's hand.

Pete hops the back fence. His Chucks crunch over gravel as he runs up the alley. That gun feels solid in his hand, but it's not the .45 that's driving him. Pete's doing that job all by himself now. The way he sees it, tonight's his only chance at a fresh start, and he's going to grab it.

You want to put a tiger in your tank, that'll do the job. Our buddy Pete's all gassed up and ready to go. You remember how that feels. It's been a long time for you, but you can't forget, not once you've made the Run on Halloween night. So you've got a pretty solid idea of the tracks Pete's laying down as we follow him up a dark street that heads out of Jerry Ricks's neighborhood. That boy's motoring, all right, but he can't keep our pace.

Not now, not where we're going. Which is straight out of town, like a witch riding a broomstick. We leave our buddy Pete in the dust, whipsawing through the poor side of town and across the tracks, flying so low that the painted line on that black asphalt smears into a yellow streak that marks the whole town for a coward. We pass that movie theater with the Vincent Price double-bill. We blow by that old brick church in the town square. Like a wild stitch of midnight we weave through a crowd of teens prowling Main Street, and they look straight at us but don't see more than a ripple of shadow and the swirling twist of a dust devil it leaves behind.

Autumn leaves and candy wrappers and wax-paper Bazooka Joe comics churn in the night. And now the town is behind us, and we're racing down the licorice-whip road. By the time that dust devil stops swirling on Main Street, we're a mile away.

Rows of dead cornstalks on each side of the road blur by like a crop of bones. There's something up ahead in the middle of the road, something that's pulling away even as we gear up the night's own tach and close on it.

A pair of coal-red brake lights glow in the rusty ass-end of that thing.

A pair of dead-white headlights glare up front, raking the blacktop like a Gorgon's stare.

Yeah. Mitch Crenshaw's rattletrap streetrod is dead ahead, chewing a hole through the night. But that doesn't cut any slack with us. Pedal hits metal that isn't even there. In a flicker of moonlight, we're even with the Chrysler's rear bumper. Another second and we're eyeballing the driver's side window.

The window's down. Inside, Crenshaw's got a fistful of steering wheel and a brain crawling with pissed-off spiders. He sucks the last drag from a cigarette and flicks it into the night. . . .

The cig sails through the window and kicks up a hail of sparks as if hitting something solid out there in the darkness, but Mitch Crenshaw doesn't pay any attention to that. He knows there's nothing outside his window but the night, and a shitload of dead cornstalks, and a pumpkin-headed monster he's ready to carve up for Halloween pie.

So Mitch does what he does best—he hits the gas and drives straight ahead. He flicks the headlights to high beam, and they cut the belly right out of the sky, and he races along the gash feeling like a guy who's just about to butt heads with his very own destiny.

Which is exactly what he's gonna do. And, in this case, Mitch knows that destiny doesn't stand a chance. The way Mitch figures it, he's the only guy in town who's smarter than the average bear. Being behind the wheel of the only car on this road proves that. This year, Mitch has it all figured out and—

"Slow down, Mitch," Bud Harris says. "You ain't gonna have a chance to kill the Boy if you kill us first."

"Yeah." It's Charlie Gunther now, chiming in from the backseat like a goddamn alarm clock. "Ease off, buddy. You keep the hammer slammed and we're liable to miss the whole damn field, let alone Ol' Hacksaw Face—"

"We ain't gonna miss nothing," Mitch says sharply, and his booted foot stays right there on the gas. Because he knows he's right, and he's not afraid to say it. Not tonight. Not when he's been locked up in his room for five days without a thing to eat. Not when hunger's burning a hole in his belly and his brain is clicking away overtime.

No. There's no room for argument on Mitch's agenda. Tonight the Run belongs to him. It's *his* game. His second crack at the October Boy, and this time he's going to get it right. Mitch doesn't really count last year, anyway. Last Halloween, he was just two days past his sixteenth birthday. He didn't even have a driver's license. But this year, things are different. This year he's seventeen, and he's got the Chrysler and a switchblade knife and some other dangerous implements in the trunk that'll spell *T-R-O-U-B-L-E* for anyone who gets in his way. But best of all, he's got the whole deal figured out good.

"Hey, I ain't kidding," Charlie says from the backseat. "I think we missed the field. We better turn around, or someone's going to beat us to the Boy—"

"Didn't you hear me the first time?" Mitch snaps. *"We didn't miss the goddamn field.* And no one's going to beat us to nothing. I mean, have you ever even heard of anyone doing what we're doing tonight? You ever hear of anyone jumping the Line?"

"No, Mitch . . . but—"

"No *buts,* stupid. I've got it all figured out. Those other dipsticks always treat the Run like it's a game of hide 'n' seek. They hang around town, waiting for the Boy to come after his *ollie ollie oxen free.* They don't bust the city limits. But that ain't the way we're gonna play it tonight. We're gonna take the Run straight to our buddy Sawtooth Jack, and

I'm gonna splatter his ass before he even gets a chance to step across the Line."

"But what if it don't work? What if the Boy gets past us somehow?"

"You know, Charlie, there are two little words that can get your ass kicked out of this car. One of them is *what,* and the other is *if.*"

Mitch shoots a glance at the rearview, eyeballing the dope in the backseat. Charlie's sitting there with a Mighty Thor comic book rolled up in his hands, and he looks like he just got whacked over the head with the big guy's hammer. And that's the way Charlie *should* look as far as Mitch is concerned. The way Mitch sees it, tonight you can screw *what if* . . . and second guesses, too. There's no room on Mitch's plate for any of that. He's up for a one-course meal, and that means winning the Run. Then everything will be different for him. Sure, the town will get what it wants—what it needs to get through another year of raising prize crops from the same old dirt, what it needs to turn those crops into cold hard cash—the whole deal delivered with a king-size platter of blessings from above or below, depending on who the hell you listen to.

Mitch sees it this way: You can screw the blessings, wherever they come from. He doesn't have a clue how anyone could settle for a life in this nothing little place, and he won't need one after tonight. Not after he bashes that living Jack o' Lantern's head into the pavement and carves those candy bars out of its woven-vine chest. That happens, the whole damn town can bury their favorite spook story in the bottom drawer and forget about it for another year, the way they always do. Until the calendar flips a bunch of pages and another crop gets picked and shucked. Until another pumpkin starts growing in that same dead field. Until someone drives out there one night, hammers together a cross, and nails up an empty suit of clothes for a fresh tangle of growing vines to fill.

But Mitch Crenshaw will be long gone by the time that happens. Once he nails Ol' Hacksaw Face, things will be different for him. Once he eats himself some of the candy that serves up a heartbeat, there won't be anyone to stand in his way.

Yeah. Bring down Sawtooth Jack, and he'll be the winner. And that'll mean a whole hell of a lot . . . both for him and his family. The family will get treated differently around town. They'll get a new house, a new car. They won't see a bill for a year—not at the grocery store, no mortgage payments, nothing. That'll make Mitch's old man particularly happy. But Mitch doesn't care about his hard-ass father, or his shrew of a mother, or his little snot sisters.

No. Mitch pretty much just cares about himself, and what winning the Run will get him. Do that and he'll grab a pocketful of green, just like Jim Shepard did last year. Even better, he'll be on this road again, headed out of town like a bullet, and for the very last time. Guys like Charlie and Bud, they couldn't even handle that. Wouldn't want to win. Wouldn't want to see their hometown in the rearview. Wouldn't know what to do if they could. Hell, they'd probably break down in tears, run screaming for mommy and daddy if someone kicked there asses across the Line for good.

That's why those guys aren't built to win the Run. But Mitch is. Winning the Run is the only way to get out of this squirrel cage of a town, and Mitch wants it so bad he can taste it. Hunger burns in his belly and burns in his brain. He wants that money in his pocket, wants everything that comes with it. Wants the town in his rearview. Wants to see what's down that black road, and across those dead fields, and out there in the world.

So that's Mitch's game. You remember how it feels, don't you? All that desire scorching you straight through. Feeling like you're penned up in a small-town cage, jailed by cornstalk bars. Knowing, just knowing, that you'll be stuck in that quiet little town forever if you don't take a chance.

So you know what it's like to want to fly down that road and see what lies beyond it . . . to want that so bad, you'll do just about anything to make it happen. Sure. You remember Mitch Crenshaw's game, the same way you remember that it isn't the only one running tonight. Glance over at the side of that black road and you'll see undeniable evidence of that. Might not be any little guy standing there in a black suit to set up the story for you, the way there is every Friday night on TV. But like that little guy says damn near every week, *there's a signpost up ahead,* even if it ain't a hunk of metal you can touch. It's written on the darkness, and it tells us that we've got a few hard miles of prime-time *Twilight Zone* action ahead on this road tonight.

Picture if you will: The flipside of a game played by a pack of teenage hoodlums in a rusty Chrysler. It's a solo B-side for a thing born in a cornfield, a requiem for the shambling progeny of the black and bloody earth. Because the October Boy has his own game. It's played with pitchforks and switchblades and fear, and its first scrimmage is set to begin on a quiet strip of two-lane that marks the midnight trail to town. For this creature with the fright-mask face is both trick and treat. He comes with pockets filled with candy, and he carries a knife that carves holes in the shadows, and his race will take him from a lonely country road to an old brick church that waits dead center in the middle of a town square . . . in The Twilight Zone.

Uh-huh. That about covers it, if you want the teaser. Hang around for thirty minutes and we'll give you the payoff. And the show can kick into gear right about here:

The October Boy spots the Chrysler's Gorgon headlights about a mile off, but he doesn't freeze. He makes for the side of the road and ducks into a clutch of cornstalks that close around him like a skeletal fist. He stands there with the butcher knife vined in his gnarled grasp, waiting as those lights grow larger . . . thinking . . . planning . . . and his thoughts aren't so different from those of the boy behind the Chrysler's wheel, because the October Boy has his own game to play, and its played with a deck that's stacked against him.

Yeah. If there's one thing the October Boy knows, it's that. But he doesn't have another way to go tonight. He's already crossed the starting line, and there's nowhere to head but the finish, though he can't imagine how he'll get there. It seems impossible. How he'll make it from this spot into town, and how he'll run the teenage gauntlet that's itching to chop him down like a two-legged weed, and how he'll reach that finish-line church in the town square before the steeple bell tolls midnight . . . well, it's gotta be the longest of all long shots.

It never happens that way.

Everyone in town says it can't happen that way.

But the October Boy has to make it happen that way.

If he wants to win.

So the Boy thinks about how he'll play it. Not long-range, but step by step. He hears the Chrysler's engine now, hears too the cool October breeze rushing in the car's wake as the Chrysler speeds through dead corn a quarter mile away.

He sucks a breath through his arrowhead nose and steadies himself. The car's coming fast. Forget miles . . . we're talking yards, now . . . and the October Boy's already moving. He slips free of that cornstalk fist, clutching the knife in his hand . . . racing through the ditch and up the incline . . . severed-root feet scrabbling over blacktop as he hits the road and crosses the white line.

The Boy's head swivels as the Chrysler closes on him. He strains for a glimpse of the driver's face through the windshield, but the window's as black as the night. The Boy can't see anyone behind it.

His carved eyes flicker in the darkness.

The dead-white headlights don't flicker at all.

Mitch jerks the steering wheel hard to port, just missing a king-sized puppet scrambling across the road. Even as the Chrysler slips into a skid he's cursing his capacity for instinctive response, because he realizes a second too late that puppet had a big orange head and hitting it head-on would have hammered flat every challenge this night holds as surely as a Sonny Liston right cross.

He doesn't have one idea about the right thing to do. That bottomless hunger churning inside him has jacked his response time around but good. So he hits the brakes, because he hates indecisiveness. The wheels lock up, and the car keeps spinning, but it doesn't go far. When it comes to a stop the rear wheels are on the edge of the road, just short of the ditch. The headlights are still trained on blacktop, only now they're aimed in the direction of the town.

As far as Mitch can see, there's not a damn thing between the Chrysler's front bumper and Main Street.

The headlights reveal nothing but road.

There's no walking nightmare in sight.

"Where'd he go?" Charlie asks.

"Has to be in one of those cornfields," Bud says.

"Or maybe we hit him," Charlie says. "Could be the whole thing's over. Could be all we have to do is find out where he dropped and shovel him into a bag."

"No," Mitch says. "I didn't hit shit. Nothing's over."

Mitch is out of the car before the words are out of his mouth. He slams the driver's side door. A second later, he's keyed the trunk and popped it. Bud and Charlie are standing at his side now, but he doesn't even shoot a glance their way. They know what they're supposed to do.

Mitch hands Charlie a big flashlight.

Bud gets a rusty pitchfork.

Mitch takes another.

Twin headlight beams stretch through the night like spun glass, but the car's not moving. Not now. From his hiding place in the dead corn, the October Boy sees three guys coming his way. One of them carries a pitchfork down the middle of the road; in the headlight glow he looks like a man walking the length of a freshly blown bottle. Behind him, a dimmer light bobs through the darkness at the road's shoulder. Two silhouettes trail along behind that solitary beam, so close that they melt into a shadowy pair of Siamese twins—a pitchfork in its left hand, a flashlight in the right.

The October Boy clutches his knife, waiting, listening.

"The Chrysler's skid marks start here," says the guy standing in the road. "See if there are any footprints down in that ditch."

Boots kick through a tangle of weeds. The Siamese twins work their way down the berm, heading toward the October Boy. "Shit, this is slippery." A splash through a puddle, and more cussing. And finally an old beer can crumples underfoot as the flashlight beam slides over the ground, marking a trail that leads from the side of the road to a break in the cornstalks.

"These don't look like any footprints I've ever seen," one of the twins says, "but *something* sure as hell ran through here."

The guy walking the road doesn't say a word. He's standing in the darkness now. The Chrysler is a good distance behind him, and so are its headlights. That pleases the October Boy, because it means it'll be tough going if these guys make a run for the car . . . especially if they have something chasing their tails that means business.

The kid in the road kneels.

"Hey," he says. "Shine that light over here."

The flashlight beam skitters across the blacktop and finds something waiting there.

The October Boy's carved teeth chew over a grin.

The boys have found the bait.

Mitch drops his pitchfork, snatches up an Oh Henry!, and rips into it. A couple quick bites and he's got the whole damn candy bar in his mouth. He chews desperately, salivating like a son of a bitch, his jaws snapping together as if he's trying to murder that hunk of chocolate before it starts crawling around in his mouth.

One hard gulp and a sticky lump of sugar makes a beeline for his belly. That sugar hits his stomach like a lightning bolt tossed by Mighty Thor himself. Man oh man. Five days with nothing to eat. Mitch doesn't know how he managed to live through that, but he's intent on making up for lost time now.

He isn't the only one. Bud's pitchfork is planted in soft ditch dirt. He's on his knees in the mud, polishing off a couple of Clark bars he found down there. And Charlie's ahead of both his pals. He's filling his pockets at the same time he's gobbling an Abba-Zaba. He's working the flashlight with one hand, following the beam into that break he spotted in the cornstalks, picking up candy as he goes along.

Mitch wants to warn the doofus, but he's got another Oh Henry! in his mouth and can't say a word. He's got to say something, though. After all, Mitch has a plan, and he needs Charlie. Charlie's the guy with the flashlight. It's his job to spotlight the October Boy while Mitch and Bud pin him to the ground with those pitchforks. That's when they're supposed to get the candy—when the Boy's helpless, when Mitch can go to work on him with the switchblade and take the time to do the job right. Carving his orange skull until the light spills right out of it. Slicing through ropes of green innards until all that gutted candy falls to the ground, and they can chow down without watching their backsides.

Yeah. That's the way it's supposed to happen: kill first, eat later. But it's no surprise that Mitch really can't help himself any more than the others. He's so damn hungry, and the candy tastes so damn good. Still, he knows he has to get a grip on things. He swallows hard, says, "Hey, that's enough, guys. We gotta be careful—"

"Yeah," Bud says. "You're right, Mitch."

Charlie doesn't say anything.

Charlie has already disappeared into the corn.

Charlie hears Mitch yelling, but that doesn't slow him down. He's ten feet into the field. There's a narrow trail pushing through the dead stalks, and up ahead he spots a heavy sprinkling of Atomic Fireballs and Candy Corn. Hell, it isn't exactly a trail of blood, but in this case Charlie's pretty sure that it means the same thing.

The flashlight beam plays over the narrow path. Charlie follows along behind it, picking up those Atomic Fireballs as he goes. He's starting to wish he'd brought a sack with him. And he's starting to figure that Mitch has gotta be wrong about missing the October Boy with the Chrysler. Gotta be. Because Ol' Hacksaw Face is losing candy like a busted piñata, which is about what you'd expect if a walking tangle of vines went head to head with a hunk of Detroit steel going eighty miles per.

The more candy Charlie finds, the more he's convinced of that. Any second now, he expects the flashlight beam to reveal what's left of Sawtooth Jack there on the ground, dim light flickering in his busted-up noggin, a thick patch of mushed Bit-O-Honeys and Red Vines staining his shirt.

But that's not what Charlie sees up ahead. Not at all. In fact, it's not what he sees that's important. It's the smell that hangs in the air that counts. And it's not chocolate, or caramel, or marshmallow filling, but an odd mix of scorched cinnamon, gunpowder, and melting wax.

There's a soft rustle behind Charlie. As he turns, he's certain he's going to see Mitch or Bud catching up to him, but you've already figured out that isn't what's creeping up on him out there in that cornfield.

Hey, that's no surprise, because you're a whole lot smarter than our buddy Charlie, aren't you?

Tell the truth now—who the hell isn't?

The kid with the flashlight is wearing a leather jacket and motorcycle boots, but the October Boy can tell right off that he's not tough at all. The little punk nearly screams bloody murder as the Boy lays the well-honed edge of the butcher knife against his jugular.

But the kid doesn't scream. He knows better. He barely whimpers. The October Boy's razored grin glows fiercely, a tiger-stripe of yellow light spilling across his wicked maw. The man with the knife had tried to muzzle him, but the October Boy isn't muzzled anymore. The Atomic Fireballs the man stuffed into his hollow head are gone now. The Boy spit every one of them onto the trail. He can speak again, and the words that cross his carved teeth are so simple and direct that even an idiot like Charlie Gunther can understand them.

"Give me the flashlight," the October Boy says.

His voice is sandpaper and battery acid. Charlie does what he's told, and right away. Back there on the road, Mitch is calling his name, but Charlie doesn't dare answer him. Even so, the October Boy's knife stays right there against his throat. Charlie feels his blood pounding against it, and the thing standing in front of him keeps right on smiling as Mitch yells louder and louder and louder.

"Don't listen to him," the October Boy says. "Listen to me."

Charlie starts to nod, but he's afraid he'll cut off his own head if he does. And his fears aren't misplaced—that knife blade presses harder, imprinting a deeper furrow in Charlie's flesh. And the knife's not even the worst of it. As far as Charlie's concerned, that prize goes to the monster's voice, which works over Charlie like some radioactive sandstorm in a sci-fi movie.

"You're going to do exactly what I tell you."

"Uh-huh," Charlie says. "I'll do anything."

The October Boy steps back, taking the knife with him.

He shines Charlie's flashlight at the road.

The instructions he gives aren't complicated.

He says, "Run."

"Maybe we should get the car," Bud says. "We can drive it down here, aim the headlights where we want to. That way we can see what the hell we're doing until Charlie drags his ass out of that field."

Mitch shakes his head. No way. He's not walking all the way back to the car, not with Charlie vanishing like the goddamn Invisible Man. That would put him a couple hundred yards up the road, and Bud right here, and Charlie god knows where. Splitting up like that wouldn't be smart.

So he yells Charlie's name. Loud. For the fifth goddamn time.

For the fifth goddamn time, he doesn't get an answer.

"That dipstick." Mitch sighs. "I should have left him back in town—"

And just that fast there's a sharp *snap crackle pop* of activity up ahead of them. It sounds like an avalanche of busting bones out there in the cornfield. Something bursts through the cornstalk wall on the other side of the drainage ditch. It crosses that dark furrow and is up on the road before Mitch can even close his yap, and it hits the blacktop running just as the cornstalks crackle again and a second figure emerges from the field like a misplaced shadow holding a flashlight—

And the running thing's closing on Mitch. The first thing out of the chute. The thing without a flashlight. Mitch grabs his pitchfork. From the side of the road, the pursuer's flashlight beam skitters through the darkness and plays into Mitch's eyes, and then it's erased by that front-running pocket of midnight heading straight for him, and he cocks the fork over his shoulder like a javelin, and he lets that sucker fly—

"Mitch, don't!"

—and the running thing catches all four teeth square in the chest—

"Mitch! Jesus Christ!"

—and that's Bud's voice, coming from behind. But Bud can't see what the hell's going on from his position. Mitch is sure of that, the same way he's sure that he hit what he aimed at, because the thing is staggering across the road now, nearly dead on its feet. And so he can't figure out why Bud is pushing past him, ready with his own pitchfork, which he sends whistling through the night with a short, sharp grunt of effort.

It sails over the head of the thing Mitch speared, straight at the figure holding the flashlight.

Mitch shouts a warning: "Charlie! Get out of the way!"

The holder of the flashlight steps to the side, dodging the tossed fork, and Bud's weapon clatters over the blacktop.

The figure turns off the flashlight just that fast.

Its triangle eyes glow in the darkness.

So does its sawtoothed grin.

Oh, shit, Mitch thinks. *Oh, shit.*

He looks down, at the thing lying in the road between himself and the October Boy.

There's Charlie, crumpled on the ground with four steel spikes buried deep in his chest.

For a second, it's quiet.

The stars shine down. The wind doesn't even whisper.

Then the October Boy bends low and picks up Bud's pitchfork. Mitch yanks his switchblade, thumbs the release, and starts to backpedal as the blade *snicks* alive in the night. He knows he can't panic. Maybe he doesn't need to panic. He's still got the knife, and Bud's got one, too. That means the odds are still two to one and—

Behind him, there's another chorus of *snap crackle pop*. Mitch whirls. Bud's nowhere in sight, but you can still hear him, plowing a path through the cornfield, running away—

The son of a bitch! He ditched me!

But Mitch doesn't have time to worry about Bud. The October Boy is advancing. Mitch is on the retreat. You can't really blame him. He doesn't think much of putting down money on a one-on-one switchblade/pitchfork rumble with a monster. Not when he's still got a set of car keys in his pocket. And not when he's got twenty feet of blacktop on the October Boy.

Yeah. He can make it to the Chrysler before Sawtooth Jack catches up to him. Sure he can. He moves fast, careful to keep those twenty paces between them, because the Boy has that pitchfork. Mitch wants to have plenty of time to get out of the way if the Boy throws it. But now Mitch has retreated far enough so that he's in the glow of the Chrysler's headlights . . . and that means he's one hell of a target. And he can't keep backpedaling, either, because suddenly the October Boy's starting to close the gap.

The hell with this, Mitch figures. *I'll take my chances. I'll get myself pointed in the right direction and launch my ass like a Mercury rocket.*

And he does just that. He turns, and his legs start pumping, and he runs for the light. And he's smart. He doesn't look back. He's not going to take that chance, because he doesn't want to see that goddamn monster closing on him with a nightmare stride that's Wilt Chamberlain times two . . . doesn't want to see the grim light spilling out of its hacked-up head like some crazy-quilt headlight as it freight-trains his ass . . . doesn't want to do anything but pick 'em up and put 'em down 'til he's safe and secure behind the wheel of the Chrysler, knifing the key into that thick neck of a steering column, twisting it sharply as his foot pile-drives the gas and he peels out, leaving five bucks worth of rubber there on the road . . . slamming that running nightmare head-on . . . threshing its scarecrow ass like a big old combine . . . grinding it under his Firestones until nothing's left but a smear of pumpkin and chocolate on the two-lane blacktop.

Uh-huh. That's what Mitch Crenshaw wants. He's halfway to the car now, holding on to his resolve like a relay runner's baton. He's not going to look over his shoulder no matter what. But as it turns out, he doesn't have to, because he's got a handful of senses besides the one attached to his eyeballs, and they tell him exactly what's going on behind him.

First Mitch's ears do the work: He hears the crazy whiskbroom sound of the October Boy's feet brushing the road . . . and then that even rhythm hits another tempo and changes up.

A couple of quick severed steps. . . .

A staccato rasp of physical effort. . . .

And then Mitch's body takes over and does the sensory work. A hot spike of pain spears the back of his right ankle, ripping a path that notches bone, breaking skin as it exits his ankle and drives down through his boot and the foot inside it. The damage is done by one of four rusty spikes attached to a pitchfork, and for an encore it punctures the sole of Mitch's boot and strikes blacktop so hard that the metal shaft rings inside his skin, and he topples in a scream of pain.

The switchblade flies out of his hand. The road comes up and whacks him like a black tsunami. Mitch's scream evaporates as the wind is knocked out of him, and he sucks a deep breath, and another scream is right there filling up his mouth, because the pitchfork's heavy handle is levering as gravity drives it earthward, and that metal spike is twisting simultaneously in Mitch's ankle and his foot.

The wooden handle slaps the roadbed, sending another sharp vibration through the pitchfork. Mitch nearly blacks out. He bites his lip and rolls onto his side. It's a hell of a mess. A rusty spike has torn a couple holes in him, and just for gravy one of the spike's neighbors is locked around the inside of his ankle and his foot. He knows he should yank out the fork and try to stand, but he can't seem to get moving any better than a turtle that's been rolled on its back.

And that's not the worst of it. The October Boy is standing about fifteen feet away, right in the middle of the road, staring straight at him. The Chrysler's Gorgon headlights reveal the thing clearly . . . just as they reveal the gleaming butcher knife that feeds stiletto-style through the knotted vines that comprise its left hand, filling it as long fingers wrap around its hilt.

And, seeing that, you know exactly how Mitch feels. He's belly to the ground, staring up at a legend. It's like staring up at Santa Claus, or the goddamn Easter Bunny . . . but only if Santa was the kind of guy who'd strangle you with your own stocking, and only if the Easter Bunny was the kind of rabbit who'd stomp you dead and peel your cracked skullcap like a hardboiled egg.

Yeah. You remember how it feels to go nose to nose with a legend. That's why the stories they spin about the October Boy are all about fear. You heard them around a campfire out in the woods when you were just a kid, and they were whispered to you late at night in your dark bedroom when your best friend spent the night, and they scared you so bad tenting out in your backyard one summer night that you thought you wouldn't sleep for a week. So there's not much chance of separating *reputation* from *reality* when you look the real deal straight in the face. He's the October Boy . . . the reaper that grows in the field, the merciless trick with a heart made of treats, the butchering nightmare with the hacksaw face . . . and he's gonna *getcha!* That's what they always told you . . . he's gonna *getcha* so you know you've been *got*!!!!!

Just ask Mitch Crenshaw if you've got any doubt about that. Because the October Boy's stalking toward him now, and there's a mutant fire glowing behind his eyes that looks like it could melt the lead lining off a bomb shelter door. That fire . . . it's bottled-up Hiroshima . . . it's 150-proof Nagasaki . . . and there's so much more to it than what it is, or what Mitch believes it to be, that he can barely stand to look at it.

Mitch closes his eyes for just a second. He tries to move, but can't. He hears the October Boy's whiskbroom footsteps, and for him that's the only sound in the world. There's nothing else out there in the night. Bud is gone. Charlie's dead at the side of the road; he'll never make another sound.

Those last two realizations get Mitch moving. He grabs the pitchfork handle and yanks. The spike exits foot and leg in an electric jolt of pain. If he can use the fork to stand up, that's a start. The Chrysler's right behind him. If he makes it onto his feet, he can lean against the hood, maybe balance that way, maybe even manage to defend himself and—

The October Boy tears the pitchfork out of Mitch's hands. He cracks the pommel of the butcher knife against Mitch's jaw. Again, Crenshaw goes down hard, his spine ratcheting against the Chrysler's front bumper as his ass finds its blacktop destination. The Boy squats in front of him, his eyes still blazing with that mutant fire Mitch can't even comprehend, and the blade of the butcher knife comes up and fills the space between their faces, and the October Boy's carved mouth chews over a single word.

"Keys."

It takes a second for the word to register in Mitch's brain, and then he digs his car keys out of his pocket and hands them over. The October Boy's fingers vine around them like they're a fistful of sunshine, and he stands and walks around the side of the Chrysler, and the driver's door creaks open.

"You'd better move," the October Boy says. "You're in my way."

The car door slams. The engine starts. The front bumper rattles Mitch's backbone. Jesus Christ, but Mitch moves then, away from that thresher of a bumper, out of the path of those brutal Firestones.

He's crawling across blacktop as the October Boy hits the gas. The stink of burning rubber fills the air. Mitch rolls down the embankment into the muddy ditch at the side of the road. An exhaust cloud follows him, settling low to the ground. Mitch lies there in the darkness. He doesn't look up. The Chrysler growls in the night. A wind rises, sowing through the corn as if chasing the big black machine, digging its way down the drainage ditch. Hamburger wrappers churn under its breath, but it doesn't last long.

And then it's quiet.

The stars shine down. The wind doesn't even whisper.

For a time. For a little while.

And then somewhere further down the ditch, a frog starts up. It's the first frog Mitch has heard all night. He's forgotten that there are frogs out here. And then another joins in . . . and another . . . and another . . . and it turns out Mitch isn't alone in the darkness. There are frogs all around him in that muddy old ditch. They were right here all along, clinging to the shadows like a silent audience—dozens of them, maybe even a hundred—and Mitch didn't know they were here at all, because they were smart enough to be quiet . . . smart enough to keep their little yaps shut when a two-legged legend came walking down the road. . . .

Mitch buries his face in his hands, listening to those frogs work over the silence. *Yeah . . . they're sure talking now,* he thinks, and then he laughs, because it really is kind of funny.

They don't waste any time running their mouths once their little green asses are safe.

Not when they've got something to talk about.

Not when they're telling a story. . . .

PART TWO
Lies

Of course, the story told by Mitch Crenshaw's amphibian friends is one the October Boy won't hear. He's already blown a couple miles down the black road, and he's concentrating hard, because driving isn't easy for him. His viny fingers cling too tightly to the steering wheel, and his severed-root feet are spongy on the gas and the brake. But he does all right, and in a few minutes he crosses the Line into town.

Kids are everywhere, running in packs with bows and arrows, and axe handles, and scythes sharpened for a single night's work. They're waiting for his grand arrival in the most obvious places, shadowing the city limits for the first sign of a thing that doesn't move like a man. So he jams the Chrysler's horn and guns through the first bunch of teenagers just as he hits Main Street, and they get out of his way double-quick because there's not much more they can do when a couple tons of steel growls at them like a king-size tomcat that's seriously pissed off.

Sure they move, but they don't scare easy. The October Boy's about fifty feet down Main when a rock hits the Chrysler's trunk. "Screw you, Crenshaw!" some guy shouts. "Get your chickenshit ass out of that car and onto the street!" And the Boy's carved grin stretches wide as he hears those words, because they mean things are going to work out better than he ever could have imagined. No way he could have crossed the Line this easily if he'd come into town on his own two legs. But no one recognizes him in Crenshaw's car, and that means he's got a chance of running his game all the way to the finish line.

How much of a chance, he's not exactly sure. There's a lot more to winning this game than just crossing the Line. And sure, his final destination is in sight—there's the old brick church, dead ahead. That's the place that spells *ollie ollie oxen free* for the October Boy, and if he gets there before midnight the game will end differently than it ever has before. But getting there won't be easy, because this is definitely one case where the shortest distance between two points isn't a straight line.

Seen in the bright light of an autumn afternoon, the brick church is the color of faded roses, but by moonlight those bricks are as ugly as old scars. Already, a few young men have gathered on the lawn beneath the narrow arched windows, and at least five guys are sitting on the steps leading up to the church door. They're playing a different set of odds than the guys running the streets. They're counting on the October Boy making it all the way to the church in one piece. After all, the church is the Boy's only predictable destination.

And that bet makes one thing a sure deal—the October Boy won't try to make it just yet. Right now, that would be suicide, and the Boy knows it . . . just as he knows he's going to have to find a safe place to think things over and come up with a plan. So he hangs a left turn and heads down a side street, flicking his lights on to high beam so it'll be tougher for anyone facing the Chrysler head-on to spot a pumpkin-headed driver sitting behind the wheel—

"Goddamn! It's Mitch Crenshaw's heap! Get outta the way!"

A dozen kids scatter as the Chrysler approaches. The guys in the first group wear dime-store monster masks. The ones in the second don't need masks at all—their pale, washed-out faces are scary enough, five days of hunger etched in the hollow spaces along with just enough chiseled insanity to send a shiver up the October Boy's gnarled spine.

Both gangs disappear into the shadows as the Chrysler blows by. It's no surprise that this kid Crenshaw has a hell of a rep. So does his car. That's just fine with the October Boy. If Crenshaw's rod is the steel equivalent of his own personal monster mask, he'll be happy to let it scare anyone who gets in his way.

He makes a couple more turns, working his way east, following back streets to the edge of the downtown section. Then he hangs a left on Oak Street and heads north, cruising by the market. The ham-fisted butcher stands guard out front, armed with a shotgun. That's the way it is all over town, any place that has food. The diner, the truck stop, the liquor store out by the highway—they all have guards posted. The powers-that-be want that five-day hunger scrabbling around inside every young man who's out for the Run. The only way anyone's eating tonight is if they spill the candy locked up in the October Boy's guts.

The Chrysler passes the market. There's one last streetlight on the corner ahead. Then another turn, and the October Boy's into the neighborhoods, where the streets are darker and oak branches climb high over the road, cutting off the moon and the stars.

No porch lights shine from the doorsteps of those houses. Not the electric kind, anyway. But light spills across some of those yards nonetheless—a bumper crop of carved pumpkins sit on those porches, their rough-hewn eyes trained on the streets as if watching the night's action—somebody's idea of a joke.

A lot of those Jack o' Lanterns are mashed. Hey, you remember that. It's a tradition—pass a house, bash a pumpkin. Get your blood pumping while you think about splattering the real deal. So it's easy to understand why many of the homes are already cloaked in darkness—Jack o' Lanterns splattered, candles out.

As he drives, the October Boy thinks about the people who live in those houses—the ones who've turned their children onto the streets. And he thinks about the houses themselves, and the quiet little rooms where nothing much ever happens, and the things that do happen that are never spoken of. But in the end it's not the houses themselves that matter. It's the people inside who count. So his thoughts return to those people, sitting boxed-up in their little rooms, and he thinks about the things they say and the things they keep locked up inside, and he wonders if you can still feel those people when their voices fall silent and their shadows disappear.

When those rooms are empty.

When those people are gone.

He clocks one block, and then another. A scream cuts through the night as he makes another turn. Just ahead there's a clot of silhouette on someone's front lawn, and a figure on the ground. There's another scream from the prone figure—gotta be it's a girl—and then one of those silhouettes rears back and kicks her, and laughter eclipses the sound of her pain.

The October Boy almost hits the brakes. Almost. Because girls don't make the Run . . . and if one of them is on the street tonight, God knows what will happen to her.

But the Boy ignores the impulse. He doesn't have time to be anyone's hero. That's not his role tonight.

So he forgets about the brakes.

He hits the gas instead.

Pete's running down the street, following the sound of the girl's screams when that same busted-up Chrysler speeds toward him, its front end cleaving the black ocean of night like the prow of Captain Nemo's *Nautilus* in that Disney movie.

This time Pete barely gives the car a second thought. Once he jukes to the sidewalk and gets out of its way, that is. His attention is focused elsewhere—on that scream, on the yard that it's coming from, on two guys looming over a lone girl who's flat-backed on a neatly manicured front lawn.

There's not much light on that subject. Three carved pumpkins sit on a small porch that skirts the front of the house, their wild yellow leers rippling across clipped grass. It's not exactly a spotlight, but it's revealing enough for Pete to recognize Marty Weston and Riley Blake. They're football players, beer-gut lineman, and they've both got brakeman's clubs because their fathers are railroad men. Between them, they've also got about three hundred and fifty pounds on the busted-up redhead at their feet.

"What's wrong, sweetie?" Riley asks. "No backtalk this time?"

The redhead barely manages a groan.

"Sounds like this skinny little hunk of nothing finally learned her lesson, Marty. Could be she's finally ready to shut up and get her ass indoors, where she belongs."

Weston nods in agreement. "The little bitch can scream some. I'll give her that. She wails like a Siamese cat tossed in a deep fryer."

"Uh-huh. It's damn sure better than listening to her talk, though. At least I understand what she means when she screams."

"You don't understand anything, idiot." The girl's voice is shaky, but there's some steel in it, too. "If you were smart, you wouldn't even be on the streets tonight. You'd be safe out back of your little Hicksville homes, yanking your peckers in the outhouse."

"Jesus . . . listen to that."

"See what I mean? Happens every time she talks. That's why I'd rather hear her scream."

Riley hauls back with a booted foot. Pete watches it happen in slow motion. And then he's all done watching. Without a word, he crosses the lawn, moving in on Riley fast, cracking the pistol butt against the bigger kid's skull just as Riley's foot digs into the girl's ribs.

Riley drops his brakeman's club and Pete whacks him again, and the football player nearly goes flat on his ass as he trips over the girl. But all those tire drills on the practice field have been good for something, and Riley catches his balance at the last second. He rips around, facing Pete now, shaking his big head like it's a four-slice toaster some moron jammed with a fork.

"McCormick?" Riley says, because even in the dark he recognizes the guy who clubbed him. "Pete McCormick?

Oh, you just picked one hell of a time to grow some guts, you little shit. I'm gonna bust you up but good."

"Uh-uh." Pete chambers a round and raises the .45. "I don't think you're gonna do that, Riley."

Riley stumbles back a step. "Hey! This asshole's got a gun!"

"Yeah," Weston says. "I can see that."

Weston's standing off to the side, and his brakeman's club is already in motion as the words exit his mouth. It's whistling towards Pete's head, and Weston's stepping in behind it, following the club's arc with his weight. As Pete ducks under it he sees Weston shifting his stance, already setting his feet and cocking the club for another swing while his idiot buddy's standing there slack-jawed like he's watching the whole thing on television, and Pete whirls to the side and points the gun at Weston just as the big lineman lets loose his second swing—

—and the brakeman's club nails Weston hard, cracking the football player's kneecap like a china plate. It's not the club Weston's holding, of course. It's the club Riley dropped. The redhead has it now, and Weston screams as she cracks him a second time, and he drops his club and goes down so hard and so fast that it seems someone should have yelled *timber.*

The girl's on her feet, at Pete's side in a second, the brakeman's club still in her grasp.

"Thanks," he says.

"Thanks yourself. I owed you one."

And Riley Blake's still standing there with his mouth hanging open, all two hundred and thirty pounds of him. The skinny little chick has his club. His buddy's on the ground, howling over a busted kneecap. Worse than that, a sawed-off misfit who never lets him copy the answers off algebra exams is staring straight at him with a fucking .45 in his hand, a gun he already used to dig a couple of divots in Riley's oversize skull, and Riley has the clear impression that the little bastard is picturing a bull's-eye right there on his oversize shirt.

"I don't believe this shit," Riley says, doubly stunned. "There ain't supposed to be any girls on the Run. And I never heard of anybody hitting the streets with a gun—"

"You're talking like there are rules to this game," Pete says, cutting him off. "There aren't any rules, Riley. Tonight there are only winners and losers, and you can figure out which one you are."

"But it's not *right*. She's *a girl*. And that's *a gun*."

"And this is a club." The girl steps in and cracks Riley Blake upside the head, and he topples like beef on the hoof whacked with a slaughterhouse hammer.

"How about that, asshole?" the girl asks, looming over him. "Is that *right* enough for you?"

Riley looks up at her, but he knows better than to say another word. The girl's bruises are painted with stark white moonlight. She's just waiting for an excuse to give it to him again. The way Pete figures it, it wouldn't take much. But Pete doesn't want that to happen, though he can't say exactly why. He grabs the girl by the shoulder and pulls her back. He's ready to tell her to lay off. But she twists around, and their eyes meet, and his words don't make it past his lips.

It's no surprise that there are tears in her eyes, but in this unguarded moment Pete sees straight through them. There's something behind those tears—something buried in the midnight black of her pupils that runs deep and strong—but Pete looks away from it, because it's like catching a glimpse of some stranger's naked heart, and his gut tells him it's something he shouldn't see until she wants him to.

"Let's get out of here," he says.

The girl doesn't say a word.

But when Pete moves, she follows.

Of course, Pete recognizes the girl. There are no strangers in this town.

Her name is Kelly Haines, and she's in Pete's biology class. Pete knows that much, but it's not like they've ever talked or anything. Like Pete, she mostly keeps to herself. As far as he knows, she's the only new girl to hit town in his lifetime.

Kelly's father was the only guy who ever managed to jump the Line. He was drafted during World War II, and—unlike every other G.I. from around here—he never returned to town when the fighting was over. Instead, he brought a war bride stateside and settled far from home. Probably never spoke a single word to his wife about the place where he was born. Probably never said a word to his daughter, either.

Kelly's parents were killed in a car accident last summer. Social Services in her hometown backtracked her father's war records and found her only living relatives smack-dab here. Just that fast she's living with an uncle and an aunt she never met, in a place that's got plenty of nothing unless you're crazy about corn and quiet.

That's Kelly's story.

At least, that's the way Pete heard it. . . .

So Pete and Kelly leave a pair of busted-up football players behind them. They head toward the heart of town, where there are bound to be more kids roaming the streets. That means they've got to be careful. Handling Riley Blake and Marty Weston was dicey enough—Pete doesn't want to replay that encounter with a larger roster of opposing idiots. Even with the .45, he wants to steer clear of trouble, and he knows he'll get it with a capital *T* if anyone catches a girl outside on the night of the Run.

So Pete and Kelly bury themselves in the shadows whenever they spot a gang on the prowl. Or they duck into an alley, or hide behind an unlocked backyard gate. In spite of the detours, the two cover some ground. They pass the town market on Oak Street. The butcher is staked out by the front door with a sawed-off shotgun, and Pete nearly doubles over at the sight of all that food safe and secure behind those big glass windows. Just looking at it makes him feel like someone tied a knot around his middle and yanked it tight.

But he knows they'd better hustle along, same way he knows that he's got nothing to complain about if he measures his misery against Kelly's. And she's not complaining at all. She's limping a little bit, but it's not like it's her leg that's hurt. The way she's breathing tells Pete that it's something else, probably her ribs. That's no surprise—she took some pretty brutal kicks.

"You need to catch a breather?" Pete asks. "We can find a place and rest up."

"I'm okay. I can make it."

"I'm not so sure."

Kelly stops and looks at him. Dead straight in the eye, like she's trying to see inside his skull, the same way he looked at her a few minutes ago.

Her eyes are green. He hadn't noticed that before.

"It's Pete McCormick, right?"

"Yeah. Right. I can tell I made a real impression on you in Bio."

"Don't sell yourself short, Pete." She smiles and lets it linger. "Maybe you did make an impression . . . and maybe you set it in cement tonight."

Pete's glad she smiled. Glad, too, that she said what she said.

"And maybe you're right about catching a break," she says. "My ribs are killing me. If we can find a place—"

And then it's like someone bashed a hammer straight through the night. A window shatters behind them. Pete whirls as a shotgun blast rocks the street, just in time to see a kid who's holding a brick get blown out of his sneakers in the grocery store parking lot.

Kelly's breath catches in her throat. Pete yanks the .45. The butcher, Mr. Jarrett, jacks another shell into his shotgun. The market's burglar alarm is ringing like it's the 3:15 bell and school just let out. Another kid charges Jarrett, and the sawed-off thunders and damn near cuts the guy in half, but there are three more kids waiting behind the two who are dead. Two of them wind up and fire bricks at the butcher. Jarrett dodges one of them but not the other. It belts him hard and he goes through a window, the busting glass cutting him in a dozen places, but he's already rolling with that shotgun as the kids move forward. The barrel rises beneath Jarrett's bloody face, and a couple more bricks hurtle in his direction, and the shotgun spits fire.

"We'd better move," Pete says, and Kelly's already doing it. Together, they run up Oak Street. Kelly's not limping now, though if you listened to her breathe, you'd know she should be. Behind them, the burglar alarm's banging in the night, and those boys are yelling like wild dogs, and Jarrett's screaming, and it's the most awful sound Pete has ever heard in his life. It's a sound that should be buckled up in a straightjacket.

Then there's another sound. A police siren. A block ahead, a black-and-white Dodge makes the corner. Pete freezes dead in his tracks. He's standing there in the middle of the street with a stolen .45 in his hand, and there's the worst kind of trouble he can think of behind him and a prowl car up ahead, maybe with the owner of that stolen pistol behind the wheel.

Headlights scorch Pete's retinas. "This way!" Kelly shouts, grabbing his arm, and Pete starts to move. But he can't escape those scorching headlights. They're tracking him as he crosses the street, and so is the prowl car.

Tires scream in the night. The stink of burning rubber fills the air. The car door bangs open. Jerry Ricks's voice chews Pete's heels. "Freeze, you piece of shit!"

That's the last thing in the world Pete's going to do. He's running along the railroad tracks, following Kelly down a raised strip of roadbed. Gunfire erupts behind them, and one of the slugs rings against the ribbon of steel just inches from Pete's foot. He grabs Kelly, yanking her toward the far rail. Another shot whips past them as they dive into the darkness. They hit the ground hard and tumble down the gravel embankment on the far side of the tracks, but Pete comes up fast with the stolen .45 in his hand.

He stays low, sticking to the shadows, watching the headlight glow spilling over the raised roadbed, waiting. . . .

Ricks's footsteps crunch gravel on the other side of the tracks. Backlit by the prowl car, the lawman's shadow stretches across the roadbed, creeping over the building at Pete's back. Pete swears under his breath. It's already too late to make a run for it. Kelly's still on the ground, and he won't leave without her . . . so it looks like he's going to have to stand his ground and—

In the distance, Jarrett's shotgun thunders again. God knows who's got the damn thing now, because the butcher's screaming like a guy who's been skinned alive, and the sound of laughing boys does the same job on the night.

Twenty feet away . . . maybe thirty . . . Jerry Ricks cusses a blue streak.

"You just got lucky, McCormick!" he yells. "That's right! I saw you, asshole . . . and I saw your little girlfriend, too! Right now I've got other fish to fry, but I'll settle up with the both of you before this night's over!"

The cop's footsteps set a brittle rhythm as he runs to the prowl car.

The door slams. The big Dodge peels out.

Pete jams the .45 under his belt and helps Kelly to her feet.

"Okay?" he asks.

"Doesn't matter," she says. "Let's get out of here."

They follow the tracks about a quarter mile.

Pete can't help looking over his shoulder, but no one's behind them now.

Before long, a half dozen hard pops of pistol fire sound in the distance. Instantly, Pete pictures those last three kids going face down in the parking lot outside the market, and Jerry Ricks standing over them with a smoking pistol in his hand.

"That's it for those guys," Kelly says, as if she's reading his mind.

She moves away from the tracks, cutting between a machine shop and a storage building owned by the railroad. Pete follows her into an alley that runs east-west. Without a word, they cut back toward Oak Street. The buildings are two-story here—square, brick and stone. Heavy cornices cut off the moonlight, but there are a few lights set above solid rear doors. Not one of those doors has a window, and most of them are marked with two stenciled words: DELIVERY ENTRANCE.

The alley runs parallel to Main Street, so Pete knows he's looking at the rear entrances of the town's largest businesses. He eyeballs each door as they pass, looking for a weak spot, but every one looks as solid as the last. Not that he'd trade the .45 for a million bucks with Jerry Ricks gunning for him, but right now he wishes he had a crowbar, something he could use to jimmy one of those doors.

It turns out Kelly's got something a lot better than that.

She stops at a door marked THEATER EXIT ONLY.

She takes a key from her pocket and slips it into the lock.

In all the excitement, Pete forgot that Kelly's uncle owns the movie theater. That's where he first noticed her—working behind the concession stand during the summer. He even bought popcorn from her a couple of times, though he was too shy to say anything.

Pete's pretty sure it won't work that way tonight. They're sitting in a couple of plush seats. Front row, balcony. The house lights are on, but awfully dim. Kelly's already filled a plastic bag with ice from the snack bar, and she's holding it against her ribs. She's fixed up Pete pretty well, too. Brought him a couple candy bars that he gobbled like a hungry timber wolf. Now he's working on a large Coke and a bucket of day-old popcorn. It's taking the edge off that five-day hunger, but to tell the truth Pete's thoughts aren't focused on his belly anymore.

There's only one thing he's thinking about, really.

"That son of a bitch tried to kill us," Pete says.

"Why do you seem surprised?" Kelly smiles. "After all, you broke into his house tonight and stole one of his guns."

"He couldn't know that yet."

"Well, a guy like Ricks just has one gear. Maybe it doesn't matter what you did."

"You don't have to tell me that," Pete says, remembering the beating Ricks gave him with that nightstick. "I know all about Jerry Ricks."

"Uh-uh. You might think you do, but you don't."

Pete's brow wrinkles. As comments go, that one's a blind-sider, and he remembers what the two football players said about the girl not making much sense. While Pete doesn't want to put himself in the same IQ ballpark as Riley Blake and Marty Weston, he's got to wonder if tonight's events have his brain rattling around in his head a little more than usual.

"Maybe I'm a little thick," he says. "If you're trying to tell me something, I think you'll have to spell it out."

"Okay. Let's try this—what do you know about me, Pete?"

"Well, I heard about your parents getting killed in a car accident—"

"Uh-uh. That's a lie."

"What?"

"My parents were killed, all right, but not in any accident. One night last summer, three men showed up at our house. One of them was your buddy Jerry Ricks. The other two were Ralph Jarrett and some guy named Kirby . . . I think he works down at the grain elevator.

"They all had guns—they broke in on us right in the middle of *Ed Sullivan*. Kirby shot my mom, killed her before she even knew what was happening. Dad went after him, but he never even got close. Ricks got in his way. They fought, and my dad ended up on the ground, and then all three of them started in on him—"

"Jesus."

"I tried to run, but Jarrett caught me. I think I went a little crazy . . . I know he hit me with his pistol, and I passed out for a while."

Kelly stops for a moment, swallowing hard. "When I came to, my dad was sitting in a chair. His face was a mess. Bruised, bloody . . . I could hardly make out what he was saying. Ricks and the other two were asking him questions about things I didn't understand. I remember Jarrett asking my father if he really thought he'd get away with jumping the Line. My dad said, 'Hell, I got away with it for nearly twenty years.' They all just laughed at that, and Ricks told him that he'd have to pay the price now that they'd finally caught up with him.

"My dad asked them if they were from the Harvester's Guild. I remember that. Ricks said, 'Well, we're not exactly from the 4-H.' Then he said they were taking me with them to pay my father's debt to the town. I remember what he said: 'Blood will square the deal.'

"I was looking at my mom, there on the floor in a pool of her own blood, when Ricks said those words. And then he shot my father. Just like that. That bastard stuck a pistol in my father's face, and he pulled the trigger, and—"

"You don't have to talk about it," Pete says.

"I can't talk about it. In the end, they got what they wanted. They brought me back to town and left me at my uncle's house. No one in the family told me anything. They wouldn't even talk about what happened. I was terrified. It wasn't the way you'd think it would be, even on days I managed to fight against it. It was like a sickness, the kind of feeling you'd never want inside you. And it kept crawling around in there. I couldn't sleep at night. I couldn't think straight during the day. If I wasn't thinking about things that already happened, I'd be worrying about things that hadn't happened yet. It was awful.

"I didn't start thinking straight until school started. That's when I heard about the Run for the first time. I figured that maybe I could get away. While everyone was hunting the October Boy, I could sneak out of town. It seemed like a really good idea . . . until tonight. Those two idiots cornered me, and it seemed like my whole plan was over before I even managed to make three blocks. And that's when I understood that nothing had changed—things were exactly the same as they'd been in our living room last summer when Ricks and those other two men broke through the door. All I could think about was how funny the whole thing was."

"Funny?"

"Yeah. First me, thinking I'd figured everything out. And then everyone else . . . "

Kelly stops, shaking her head.

"What?" Pete asks. "What about everyone else?"

"Every kid in this town, chasing after a boogeyman with a pumpkin for a head, scared to death of a walking scarecrow with a big sharp butcher knife. Every kid in this town, thinking that there's a way out of a nightmare through a fairy tale, when there's really no way out at all."

"You're telling me that the October Boy isn't real?"

"Oh, he's real, all right. Sawtooth Jack is out there. But I don't think he's the boogeyman, Pete. I think he's something else entirely... something that's not really that different from you or me."

Pete sits there. He's planted in a plush chair in a movie theater. He's hanging on to every word Kelly says. He doesn't even realize it, but he just grabbed another handful of popcorn, the way you do when things are getting really good. And now he's staring straight ahead at those midnight blue curtains that hang across the stage, and it's almost as if he's expecting them to pull back and reveal that big-ticket plot twist that's been hiding up there on the king-size CinemaScope screen all along—

"Who won the Run last year?" Kelly asks.

"A guy named Jim Shepard."

"And what happened to him?"

"Hell, everybody knows that. Shepard got a pocketful of money, and he got out of town. I heard he's out west somewhere, and—"

The words die in Pete's mouth just that quick. It's Kelly's knowing smile that killed them. But that's okay with Kelly. Pete's silence means his brain's finally kicking into gear.

Yeah. Pete's starting to think. Maybe he's thinking about Jim Shepard's parents, who don't seem very happy in spite of their brand-new house, and the free ride at the bank and the market, and that shiny black Cadillac parked in their driveway that doesn't even have 1,000 miles on the odometer. Or maybe he's thinking of Shepard himself, what kind of kid he was, what kind of trouble he might have caused in a town like this if he'd been bottled up here for another year and started to wise up to the way the wheels really spin.

Or maybe, just maybe, Pete's thinking about a group of men called the Harvester's Guild, and a thing that grows out in a cornfield. Maybe he's wondering what kind of horror might sprout a misfit like that, wondering too if the seed was planted last Halloween night in dirt tamped down with a murdered kid's blood—

That midnight blue curtain still covers the movie screen like a shroud, but Pete might as well be the Man with the X-Ray Eyes because he can sure enough see a movie running in his head. It's called *The October Boy,* and that sucker has just kicked off the cinches.

You know how that works, even if we're only talking *revelations* of the creepshow variety. You lay down your money, you get real comfortable in your chair, you eat your popcorn . . . and all of a sudden here comes twenty feet of cross-dressing Norman Bates heading your way with a knife in his hand, or Vincent Price pulling the strings of his killer skelo-puppet up there in the house on Haunted Hill, or that poor son of a bitch who discovered that first pod in *Invasion of the Body Snatchers*. Those are the kinds of surprises that make you jump in the dark, but you can leave them right there if you want to. The credits roll, and you suck that last sip of Coke out of your wax-paper cup and shove that empty popcorn bag under your seat along with Normie and Vince and all those rubbery pods and the guy who found them, and you walk out of the theater and down the street and back into the world where you live.

But that's not the way it works with the October Boy's story. Darkness . . . light . . . it all lives here. Real is real, no matter where you're sitting. Once you've ripped the Phantom's mask off this sucker, you're knuckle to door with the truth. You've dug a hole in that monster's ugly skin, and it's scabbed over the top of you and scarred over, and there's no way out now that you're living in the place where black blood flows.

Yeah. That's where we are right now. Pete McCormick's sitting in the movie theater, wheels turning in his head like they've never turned before. The October Boy's behind the wheel of Mitch Crenshaw's Chrysler, driving through a town he hasn't seen in exactly one year. They're a study in before and after, these two. This year's best shot at winning the Run, and last year's undisputed champ.

Because the October Boy has a name, and if you haven't already figured it out that name is Jim Shepard. One year ago on a night just like this one, Jim brought down the '62 version of Sawtooth Jack with a length of case-hardened chain. Shepard caught last year's model trying to crawl down a manhole over on West Orchard Street, cut the goggle-headed sucker off at that particular pass, and got down to the business of a no-holds-barred, one-on-one rumble.

And that was okay with good ol' '62. He'd already killed seven on his way into town that night, and he pegged Shepard for an easy number eight. So the Boy came straight at Jim with his butcher knife, and it was touch-and-go for a while. With a single slash, Ol' Hacksaw Face notched Jim's wrist to the bone. He creased the meat between a couple of Shepard's ribs with another, but that didn't even slow Jim down. He came back hard, caving in the Boy's serrated grin with a whip of the chain, turning those taut links on the follow-through and pulverizing half the thing's head.

When Jim was done wailing away, all that remained of '62 was a broken thing twitching on the ground. Yet the moment of victory wasn't the way Jim thought it'd be. It was weird . . . unsettling in a way he could never anticipate . . . like winning the Indianapolis 500 but running over his own dog to do it.

In the heat of the moment, Jim couldn't understand that feeling. But even in the heat of the moment he understood that there was no going back—once the thing was done, there was no undoing it. So he watched the October Boy twitch and die, and doing that made him go a little nuts. You understand. All those conflicting emotions slamming around inside Jim, and all at once. They had to go somewhere.

So Jim turned them loose. He raised his face to the moon and screamed. That's what the whole town wanted him to do, anyway. This year's winner was screaming in the streets, and everyone turned out to celebrate. First it was the other guys on the Run, because the dead thing in the middle of West Orchard attracted them like a raw steak draws flies. They came by the dozen, and they ripped the Boy apart and chowed down on those treats buried inside him, and they slapped Shepard on the back and raised him onto their shoulders.

And to the victor went the spoils. Someone shoved a handful of Bit-O-Honeys into Jim's hands. The candy bars were tied up in a knot of Red Vines that gleamed like blood vessels, but Jim didn't care. He peeled those Vines and gobbled them down as the guys carried him over to Main Street, not even realizing that the mass of honey-flavored candy clutched in his hand had pulsed like a human heart just a few minutes before.

The parade made its way up Oak Street, hung a right onto Main. You know the route . . . and you can see them there, even now. You see them in your mind's eye. There they are . . . the town fathers wait for Jim over in the square, the mayor and the minister stand stiff and proud on the steps of the old brick church. People crowd the streets, driving up in family sedans, hurrying in on foot from nearby neighborhoods.

Jim's dad pulls up in his old beater of a pickup truck while the mayor's glad-handing his son. Jim's mom smears tears all over her son's cheek when she hugs him, and he can't even figure out why she's crying. He can barely keep track of everything that's going on. The bell in the church tower is clanging away. Jim's little brother stands at his side in a bathrobe, still rubbing the sleep out of his eyes. The street's alive with headlights, car doors slamming, and footsteps. Rock 'n' roll's blasting from dashboard radios. Everyone's whooping and hollering. Caught up in the celebration, Mr. Haines opens up the movie theater lobby. He's giving out free popcorn and Cokes and candy, but the real show is out in the street. No one really wants to be stuck inside when there's a party like this going on.

But the party doesn't last long. Not for Jim, anyway. Soon the crowd begins to thin. That hard-ass cop, Jerry Ricks, hustles Jim and his father into the church. The mayor's inside now; so is the chief of police. The men circle the altar and tie themselves up in a little knot with the minister . . . and they trade a few words with Jim's dad . . . and all of a sudden they're leaving through the back door with Jim knotted tight in the middle of the pack, as if Houdini himself did the job and did it right.

Jim shoulders into Ricks's prowl car with the whole bunch of them. They drive across the Line. And you know how Jim feels. He can't believe it's all happening quite this fast. He's really going to get away. He's really going to get out of this nothing little town, just like that. No final speeches. No testimonial dinner. Not so much as a *kiss my ass,* really. Hell, Jim didn't even get a chance to say good-bye to his mom or his little brother. The town doc didn't even stitch up the gash in his side, or the one on his wrist. He's still bleeding, now that you mention it.

It all seems crazy. And, of course, it is. Everything around here is crazy. Jim knows that from way back. There's part of him that trusts that craziness, and it's the part that tells him this particular brand of insanity is his ticket out of town.

But there's another part—a smarter part—that tells Jim he shouldn't trust anything.

Never. Ever. Not around here.

You know which part of Jim is right. And when he finds himself down on his knees in that cornfield with the business end of Jerry Ricks's .38 pressed against his temple, Jim knows, too.

He's figured it out, same way they all do.

He's figured it out, just a little too late.

So there's poor Jim. He's finally got a clue. His knees dig divots in the dirt of that field where it always happens. The cold metal circle of a gun barrel presses hard against his gullible head. The men from the Harvester's Guild form a half-circle in front of him, while a couple of the big ones standing close to Jim's dad feed the old man that well-practiced line about *the biggest sacrifice a man can make.* And when Jim's dad finally breaks down and tries to stop the whole thing it's way too late, because those guys are built for something besides talking and they wrestle Dan Shepard to the ground and remind him that it'd be pretty easy to dig more than one grave out here tonight—with a little work, they can empty another hole . . . a smaller hole.

"Hey . . . you've got another son, don't you, Dan? Richie's ten, right? You want him to see eleven, don't you, ol' buddy?"

There's not much left after that. The preacher drones on, drawing a diagram that Jim doesn't even need anymore, getting in a few *amens* before Ricks pulls the trigger and those two big guys turn Jim's father loose to cry and babble in the dirt while they get busy with the task of digging a hole.

But, hell, I'm wasting my breath telling you about this stuff. I'm preaching to the choir. After all, you know how it feels to go face down in that hole. You've known all along. Because you're a winner, just like Jim. You've been for a ride in that prowl car. You've sat shoulder to shoulder with those men. You've had the cold barrel of Jerry Ricks's pistol jammed against the side of your head, and you've felt that .38 slug slam through your brainpan and ricochet around in your skull.

You've been buried in that black dirt. And you came through the ground the next summer, first a green shoot and then a tendril. You climbed that pole and filled those old clothes, and when Halloween rolled around you were shorn like a winter wind. Someone put a butcher knife in your hand, and you made your way to town the best way you could, and you headed for that old brick church because that's where they said you had to go.

But you didn't make it . . . we never make it. You were brought down by a kid who was just like you. And they ripped you apart in the streets while that kid screamed at the moon, and they shoveled what was left of you into a bag while that kid took a ride in Jerry Ricks's prowl car, and you rotted in a dumpster while flies circled above and the cold November sun shone down.

That's the way it is for every winner in this town.

For you. For me. For all of us.

For keeps. For always.

Yeah. It's always quiet when that first November morning dawns. Quiet through the winter, quiet through the spring. And then it starts up all over again. Summer rolls around, and the farmer who owns that black patch of earth starts watching the ground really closely, waiting for the tendril of a pumpkin plant to break through the rich soil. And when it does, he tends that sprout like a newborn babe until it takes root solidly and reaches for the sun.

He plants a heavy crosspiece in the ground. When the first vine starts to climb, he nails a set of old clothes to that crosspiece and sends the vine burrowing through them. And as the summer winds along, a thing with roots in a dead boy's corpse grows into those clothes. A vine creeps out the neck and starts to grow a head, which the farmer places on the crown of the pole. And then Halloween night rolls around, and a pale man in a new black car drives out to that field where he shed tears just a year ago, only now he has no more tears to shed. Instead, he has a job to do. So he frees the thing that used to be his son from that pole, and he carves him a face, and he sets him walking on the black road that leads to town.

It happens every year.

It happened tonight.

And now the thing that used to be Jim Shepard is driving down West Orchard in a stolen car, heading for the place he used to call home. And his father is sitting in a darkened church with a shotgun, self-loathing churning in his gut as he waits for his shuffling misfit of a son to step through the creaking door and show its carved-up excuse for a face.

And all the rest of them are out there in the darkness. The other fathers, the other sons. On the wrong side of the tracks, there's a drunk named McCormick who's wishing he'd had the guts to stop his kid from walking out the door, because he knows how smart his boy is, and he knows that he's just the kind of kid who could come out on top on a night like this one.

There's a kid named Mitch Crenshaw on the other side of the Line in a ditch, crying like a baby because his pitchforked leg and foot are really screwed up and all he can do about it is lie in the mud and bleed and whimper. And over in the poor side of town there's a kid named Weston lying on some stranger's lawn, biting back the pain of a shattered kneecap he's damn well sure won't be tended until morning. And down that street and around the next corner there's a kid named Riley who's been busted in the face with a brakeman's club, only Riley's not as smart as Weston. He's banging on his parents' door, begging to be let in, but his old man tells him he'd better get back on the streets or else he'll wind up with a couple of ounces of buckshot in his gutless belly.

And that's how the lesson is learned around here. Kids in the neighborhoods, bashing Jack o' Lanterns. Kids on the church steps, waiting with pitchforks and bowie knives. Kids in the streets, chasing shadows. And down at the market, there's a cop named Jerry Ricks and a couple of other guys loading five dead teenagers into the coroner's wagon, and a group of kids blow by the parking lot on bicycles, and they whisper, "I hear Sawtooth Jack slaughtered those guys in five seconds flat. He even killed old man Jarrett, and that dirty bastard had a shotgun that was loaded for bear. . . ."

So the story spins on. The boys on those bicycles carry it through the night, and it rides over the tracks and down Main Street, chattering away like playing cards stuck in the spokes of their bicycles.

Yeah. That's the way it works around here.

A story has to stick with those who tell it.

It belongs to them.

Just like the October Boy, it's got nowhere else to go.

And there he is, just up ahead, getting out of Crenshaw's rod, so let's let him lead the story on.

The thing that used to be Jim Shepard scrapes across the yard on severed-root feet, kicking his way through tangles of weeds as he makes his way to one of those dark little houses. But this particular house is different than its neighbors. No Jack o' Lanterns—busted or otherwise—wait on the porch. And no people wait inside.

Peeling paint scabs the front door. It isn't even locked. After all, there's nothing inside this house that anyone would want to steal. So you could say that the place is empty, but it's a special kind of empty.

It's as empty as the October Boy's hollow head.

Some would say that there's nothing in that space at all, and others would say that it's only filled with flickering light and murderous intent, but memories fill up that orange gourd as the October Boy reaches for the doorknob. There's a nasty creak as the door swings open. That's a new sound for Jim, and different. So is the sound of his whiskbroom feet on the hardwood floor—just a scratching whisper through the dust, not the strong staccato of the polished motorcycle boots he wore a year ago on the night he won the Run.

Those boots are buried in a grave with what's left of Jim's corpse, but his memories are right here with him. They're locked up in that hollow head of his, and they're locked up in this empty house, too. He wanders through the rooms quietly, step by step, and the light from his triangular eyes strips them of shadows and paints them in bright autumnal light.

In the living room, there's that heavy oak coffee table his father built by hand because he couldn't afford the ones you'd buy at a department store in the city. Same goes for that big slab of a table in the dining room, and Jim knows that if he crawled underneath it and trained a triangle of light on the wood in just the right place, he'd see his father's initials etched deeply in sanded oak, carved there by the same hand that carved the face Jim wears tonight.

Jim's misshapen fingers scrape across the rough-hewn table. It's not a good table. It sits kind of cockeyed, and dinner peas escaping a child's fork have been known to roll off the side like ships sailing off the edge of a flat earth. That's why nobody bothered to steal the thing when the house was abandoned, and Jim's glad of that. Because this is the table where he sat with his mother and father and little brother as the days faded to evenings for years and years and years. And this is the table where he thought many things, and a few of them made the trip from brain to mouth and found the ears of those other people who shared the table, but many of them didn't. For one reason or another, many of his thoughts never left him at all.

That's the way it was for Jim.

That's the way it was for his mother and father, too.

Jim never understood that before, but he understands it now, just as he understands that there's no changing the past once it ticks on by. He takes his seat at the table, and the truth of his last thought is contained in that simple act as it would be in no other.

The darkness pulls close around him. He writes his last name in tabletop dust with a fingertip, and he thinks of his family in another house. It's a new house, with a new table from one of those department stores in the city. His father sits at the head; his mother at the foot. His brother sits between them—a little older now, a little bigger. And Jim wonders what thoughts go through Richie's head as he stares at the empty chair that sits across from his place at the table, and he wonders if those thoughts ever find their way out of his little brother's mouth.

Jim thinks about that, but he doesn't think about it long.

There isn't much to think about, really.

He already understands that the past can't be changed.

Now he's beginning to understand how easily it can be repeated.

That is a hard truth—born of memory, cemented by experience. As the October Boy stares down at his name written in the dust, he feels its weight. And his gaze travels to the corded vine of a hand that wrote that name, casting a hard triangle of light on his gnarled excuse for a palm. He can feel the past there in his open hand. It's so strange, really. Because his little brother is there, within that light, and so are his parents. He feels them, too, in the glow that burns within his carved skull . . . and in the dust that coats his fingertip . . . but he can't feel himself there, not the way he was, because another thing sits in Jim Shepard's chair tonight.

If the Boy were to look in any mirrors he'd find that thing trapped within the glass. He can't escape it no matter how hard he stares, no matter what he remembers. Tonight he is a thing carved up in a cornfield, not a thing that would be welcome sitting at anyone's dinner table, not a thing that belongs in anyone's house.

He feels that as surely as he felt the knife his father drove into his face so many hours ago. But he also knows that he lived in this house. Before it became an empty shell, this place was his home. So surely he must have left some mark, some touchstone that can strengthen his resolve now. Perhaps that thing is hidden, like the initials his father carved on the bottom of the table. Perhaps it's something he'll have to look for, something that can't be found in the light, something that remains in the shadows.

And so the October Boy goes looking for a sign.

He walks to Jim Shepard's bedroom. His features are cast on the closed door like a shadowshow turned inside out—triangle eyes, arrowhead nose, sawtooth smile—and the yellow glow spills into the room as he opens the door.

Things have changed. Jim's simple desk and dresser are gone. His Spartan single bed has vanished along with its cowboys and Indians spread. Instead, an old double mattress sprawls in the middle of the floor with a couple of moth-eaten blankets tumbled across it like a hobo's nest.

The bedroom's lone window is painted black. Half-melted candles crowd the sill. Dried rivulets of colored wax stretch in frozen streams from the wall to the hardwood floor. Teenagers have carved their initials on that floor, and cigarette burns scar the dusty oak, and the butts of those cigs swim in the grimy shallows of beer bottles set adrift on the wooden sea.

It's awful, really. Horrible to come looking for yourself in a place once so familiar, and find it turned into something like this. And it isn't the destruction that bothers you, and it isn't the neglect. None of that can scrape a razor across your insides once you've endured the things Jim Shepard has endured. But there are other things here, things far worse than the stink of empty bottles and cigarettes dragged down to the filter.

Those things can't be missed, or ignored.

They're as plain as the handwriting up there on Jim's bedroom wall.

Graffiti fills that space, scrawled in paint and pen and permanent marker. Just words, only words, but to the October Boy they are so much more, for the yellow glow that spills from his head reveals the moments that put those words on the wall and the hand behind each one of them.

The front door doesn't move an inch out there in the living room, but the Boy hears it swinging open as the lock is picked on a cold night last November. The laughter of drunken jocks echoes down the empty hallway, and a pack of shadows drifts through the bedroom door. The president of the Letterman's Club pops a beer and raises it, toasting the baddest cat who's blown the block. The jocks roar their approval, cracking bottles together as a spray-paint can swiped from Murphy's Hardware hisses two huge black words across the center of the wall: SHEPARD RULES.

Beneath that sound, there's the squeal of a heavy permanent marker on a summer's night: JIM'S KING OF '62! snakes across the wall in black letters, written by a loner who spent a solid week's worth of corn-shucking money on a Levi's jacket just like the one Shepard wore the night he won the Run. And there's another kid standing next to him—he's barebacked on an August night, wearing nothing but a pair of jeans. And he can't believe he's writing JUMP THE LINE!!!!! on *this* wall while his girlfriend lies naked on the mattress behind him, drifting in a half-dream as she thinks of the things she just did in the room where Jim Shepard used to sleep.

That girl can't hide her feelings—her boyfriend might as well be a shadow as she dreams her dream . . . and pretty soon he is. A lush cornfield eclipses his face, the words WELCOME TO CORNCOB, NOWHERE threading like dark weeds through the green. Coming through that cornfield is a pumpkin-headed maniac with a knife, and if that naked girl got a look at him she'd scream her little head off. But she's long gone by the time this particular September night rolls around—Sawtooth Jack's razoring a path toward an artistic kid who's so damned scared he can barely work up the courage to draw the demonic scene stirred up in his brain . . . a kid who'll knuckle under in just a second and run into the night, leaving his art-class chalk there on the floor. And his pumpkin-headed creation will live up there on the wall as the calendar turns another page, but the chalk won't last. It'll grind to dust under a pair of heavy boots two weeks later as an angry boy with one hand in a cast cavemans a message on the wall, calling down the sadist who shattered his wrist with one crack of the nightstick.

FUCK JERRY RICKS, the wall practically screams, AND THE HORSE HE RODE IN ON.

And finally there's a quote, written as inspiration just a few nights ago. Eight words invented by a young man with too much imagination and too much faith:

AIN'T NO STOP SIGNS
ON THE BLACK ROAD.
—JIM SHEPARD, '62

Jim Shepard never spoke those words in the seventeen years he spent on earth, but the October Boy whispers them now. They cross his jagged teeth in a dizzy fury, and for a moment he staggers under their weight . . . but only for a moment.

He shakes off the weight of shadows, and the weight of those who cast them.

All those strangers are gone now, but their words still cling to the wall.

Jim reads them in the harsh yellow light, staring at his name, knowing quite suddenly that he doesn't even own it anymore.

That's right. It isn't his. Jim Shepard doesn't exist anymore. Sure, he's buried out in a cornfield, and sure, he's walking around on a pair of twisted-vine legs tonight, but nothing remains of the boy he was. What Jim had has been stolen, the same as everything else . . . stolen, and set to another purpose . . . until all that remains is a bunch of words scrawled across a wall, and those words spell out sentences that get kids drunk the same way those sweet poisons they find in bottles get them drunk.

And that's the way it works. With words, with poison. You drink those sentences down, and they prop up the dreams you keep inside you, and they spark something up there in your brain, and when you're done you've got a bellyful of the most dangerous liquor on earth.

When you're done, you've got yourself a story . . . one you can really believe.

That's what the October Boy finds in Jim Shepard's bedroom.

A story . . . *the story* . . . only it doesn't have anything to do with the real Jim Shepard, and it isn't even the truth.

It's a lie. Same as Jack and the Beanstalk, with his goose that lays the golden eggs. Same as the story about that hook-handed killer who haunts every lover's lane in every little town you ever heard of. Same as that old yarn about George Washington hacking down a cherry tree, or the tales you hear about Davy Crockett, or Billy the Kid, or Mickey Mantle.

They're all lies.

The October Boy laughs his sandpaper laugh. Take one look at him and you'd have to say that there's not much left of Jim Shepard that anyone would call human. There's only a weavework of unnatural growth topped off with a carved nightmare of a head. But rooted deep within all that is a piece of equipment that's as human as it gets. It's a gnarled collection of vines twined one 'round the other like a thing created to dull an angry fieldhand's scythe. It's a backbone, and right now it feels finer than any made out of bone and blood and muscle.

Right now it feels like case-hardened steel, like it could shatter any blade in the world.

And it will. The October Boy will stake everything he has on that. He breathes the raw stink of scorched cinnamon and gunpowder and melting wax boiled up in his own hollow head, and he tells himself it will be so. The butcher knife creeps slowly from his wrist like a demon tomcat's claw, and his fingers strangle the hilt as it fills his hand, and he promises himself that he'll slaughter that lie tonight; he'll carve the truth straight out of the shadows. He'll make it to that church before the steeple bell tolls midnight. He'll scream his *ollie ollie oxen free* so loud that everyone in town will cringe at the sound of his nightmare voice, and he'll ring that bell until the rusty clapper flies free, and God help any fool who gets in his way.

That's the way it has to be. The cycle will be broken tonight. No other boys will write on this wall, and no other boys will read the lies written there. Richie Shepard will never dream a single dream in this dead room. He'll remember his brother Jim the way he was. He'll never be touched by the sour wishes that live here, and he'll never be tempted to add one of his own to those that blacken this wall.

The October Boy will see to that. If he lives until the calendar turns a page, then the story can't. If he makes it to that church before midnight, then there'll be no winner to sacrifice, no new boy to bury out in that cornfield. If he wins, the only dead thing remaining to fill the undertaker's shovel will be the story, and that won't be enough to grow another October Boy next year.

The Boy turns his back on the lies written on his bedroom wall. It's time to go to work. His eyes spotlight the windowsill. There's a matchbook to one side of the melted candles. He snatches it up. Next come the blankets from the worn mattress, which he tumbles against the far wall.

It's hard to light a match with twisted-vine fingers.

You have to be careful.

You have to take a chance.

PART THREE
Fire

Of course, the October Boy knows what stands between him and the church. Packs of teenagers roaming the street like armed villagers in some old Frankenstein movie. Loners clinging to the shadows, ready to take off his head with baseball bats and fire axes. Young men sitting on the scar-colored brick steps of the church, waiting for their hometown's own personal Big Bad Wolf to come sniffing at the door.

The October Boy knows he can't run that kind of gauntlet. There's not enough luck in this bleak little town to see him through. And that's part of the reason he lit the fire—to create a diversion that will draw those young men away from the church, and at the same time give himself a sliver of a chance to get inside that building alive.

That's what the Boy's thinking about as flames erase the words written on his bedroom wall. He slams the door of the house he used to call home, and he slips behind the wheel of Mitch Crenshaw's Chrysler. As he keys the engine, he pictures himself kicking open the front doors of the church.

A fireball blooms in his old bedroom as he peels out. The black window explodes. Shards of broken glass stab the dead lawn. Flames sweep down the narrow hallway, spilling into the dining room, climbing the legs of the dinner table his father built, blistering wallpaper that bursts aflame.

The thing that used to be Jim Shepard doesn't see any of that. He doesn't even look in the rearview mirror. He stares dead ahead, into the night. There are other fires waiting to be lit. And there are matches in the pocket, each one of them the seed of an inferno. But the October Boy isn't thinking of fire as he hangs the corner and leaves the burning house behind. In his mind, fire is only a means to an end. His thoughts remain fixed on the church.

Seen in the cold yellow consciousness crackling within his hollow head, that building is already empty. Those who gathered around it on this blackest of nights have already turned their backs on it. That's how solidly the Boy believes in fire, and his strategy. But that strategy is flawed. For there is at least one person who won't be drawn away from the heart of the town tonight. The heat of a thousand fires wouldn't move that man from his final sanctuary, though Jim Shepard doesn't realize that yet.

No. Jim doesn't know about the man who sits in the front pew, alone in the darkness. For the powers that be—those trusted few who make up the town's Harvester's Guild—that man is an insurance policy, a last line of defense. But for the October Boy, that man is a destination—however unanticipated—as well as an individual.

He's the place where a single line connects into a circle.

Dan Shepard sits alone in the front pew, a riot gun cradled in his arms.

Jim's father stares at the cross hanging dead center on the wall ahead, but that piece of hardware has never been more than window dressing in this town. It doesn't mean much of anything to Dan, so he looks at his hands instead.

Cupped palms fill with moonlight filtered through a stained glass window. When he was just a teenager, Dan had those palms read at a carnival that passed through town. The fortune-teller told him that his lifeline was strong and his heartline was deep. But looking at his hands now, Dan doesn't remember which line was which, so he has no idea if the intervening years have changed that schematic.

He only knows that his hands hurt something awful. Been a while since he worked with a hammer, like he did earlier tonight. And he sure never did a job with a butcher knife like the one he did out in that cornfield. Carving a face for the thing that used to be his son really put the ache in him. If he had some aspirins, he'd chew them up good right now and dry swallow every bitter grain.

Not that aspirin could mask the real ache, the one that lives down deeper than the grooves scoring his calluses. No. The real pain hides beneath his heartline and his lifeline and whatever those other lines are called. It lives in his joints; it lives between his bones. And Dan knows why that ache feels at home there, though he can't quite remember how long it's been that way. All he knows is, it's a sure-enough fact that he put his hands through the mill in the years since that dark-eyed fortune-teller closed her fingers around his.

Dan always worked them hard in the fields—he did that for twenty years and then some—but he worked them harder tonight. Carving a face for his twice-born child at twilight. Then turning his back on the thing that used to be Jim and driving back to town. The way Dan sees it, that was plenty enough backbust for one evening, but it turned out it was only the beginning. Toss in a phone call from some bigwig in the Harvester's Guild a couple hours ago if you want to notch things up, add the bastard telling him he had to meet Jerry Ricks face to face if he was prepared to blow things off the dial.

Ricks. The bastard who put a bullet in his son's brain a year ago tonight. By the time Dan made it to the cop's house, the eager monster was already out on the streets—that's how impatient he was about getting his licks in tonight. So they had to meet here, at the church. That little dance was a whole different kind of torture, one Dan can't forget:

"If it was up to me, you wouldn't even be here," Ricks says, dragging on a cigarette. "I don't like the way you cringe, Shepard. I think you're the kind of man who cries in his beer."

"But you need me anyway, don't you? Because I'm the only man who can stop him if he gets this far. I'm the only one he'll listen to. You can't talk to him. If you tried to explain things to him, he'd carve out your guts with that butcher knife before you could say two words."

"Maybe, maybe not. Doesn't really matter if the Boy could slice off a hunk of me. I couldn't take him down even if I wanted to. We both know it has to be a kid brings down the October Boy. That's the only way it works. And as far as sitting that freak down and explaining the facts of life to him—well, that's sure as hell not my job."

"Yeah. I almost forgot. You're the town executioner, aren't you, Jerry?"

"Shit on that. This year I'm the goddamn exterminator. The Run's gone nuts. I had to gun down a bunch of kids over at the market. The little bastards were trying to break in. They killed Ralph Jarrett in cold blood—"

"Weeding out the strong ones, huh?"

"Just doing what needs done, asshole. I expect you to do the same. Your kid makes it through that door before twelve, you have a come-to-Jesus meeting with him. You show him he can't win this thing. You explain exactly why he has to lose.

And if he doesn't get the message, you jam that shotgun barrel against his belly and you tell him to get his ass back out there on the streets where he belongs. Because if he's not dead by midnight, this whole damn town is going straight to hell."

"You're a little late, Jer. We made that trip a long time ago."

"Keep it up, smart guy. Go ahead and act like you've got a backbone, if it'll make you feel better. You just take care of that freak if he comes walking into this place tonight. He's your responsibility. After all, you're the guy who squirted him out of the end of your dick."

Ricks smiles when he says that last part. Just a little bit. Just enough. And the words and the smile burn in Dan's brain and set his guilt on the sizzle. He nearly bites his tongue, nearly doesn't say a word. Because he's already lost one son, and he's got another one at home, and he knows exactly what Ricks and his buddies in the Guild are capable of. He knows shutting up would be the smart thing to do, but his mouth is working before his brain can dam up his words, and those words are measured and bitter when they come.

"You can't imagine what it takes. Just to sit here and talk to you. Just to do that much."

"Oh, I can imagine. One look at you, and I get a real clear picture."

"You don't see shit."

"Yeah I do. I see plenty."

"No you don't. You can't see anything, and for one simple reason."

112

"What's that, genius?"

Dan takes a deep breath, staring at the clueless bastard.

"You don't have any kids of your own, do you, Jerry?"

"Hell, no. You'd have to be nuts to have kids in a town like this."

Again, Ricks smiles, the way he smiles when he works that heavy bag in his backyard. It's as if the lawman nailed Shepard with a jab, dodged a counterpunch that had some potential hurt in it, then came back with a hammer of a right hand that shook his opponent to the core. And now he's standing there, just waiting for Dan to forget the Marquess of Queensberry and go to fucking work.

In another town, it'd happen just that way. Dan would raise that riot gun, and Ricks would draw his pistol, and in a second one (or maybe both) of them would surely hit the floor bleeding. But that won't happen here. In this town it's different. Here, Dan Shepard can't take that risk, not with a wife and kid at home. So Dan swallows those words . . . and though they're not a pleasant meal, they're nothing he hasn't tasted before.

Once he gets them down, all he can do is laugh.

It's his laughter that allows him to turn his back on Jerry Ricks.

It's his laughter that carries him inside the church.

So that was that. Dan carried Ricks's riot gun up the back steps, unlocking the back door of the church with the preacher's own key, thumb-popping his knuckles as he walked through the silence and took his place in the front pew.

And he sat there, and he waited.

And he sits there now.

No, you don't have to ask Dan Shepard about hurt. And you don't have to ask how he got here, or how he can sit in the quiet with a shotgun cradled in his arms while he waits for the thing that used to be his son. He knows why, even if the words don't cross his lips. Dan's not a stupid man.

Just because he can't put a name to the furrows life carved in his hands doesn't mean he can't see where those ditches run. He knows well enough where they run. He even knows how those ditches were dug. Hell, sometimes he can almost see the shovels working. And tonight he hears those kids screaming in the streets, and he remembers what it was like to be sixteen . . . or seventeen . . . or eighteen, and run in their number. When he could believe the things that people told him, and he could chase after a dream until his heart pounded like it was ready to batter its way through his rib cage and take off on its own.

And that's the way it was back then. For Dan and for all the guys he knew. You remember how it was, because you weren't really any different. You could believe the things that people told you, too. Their words were gospel, and you trusted them. You believed because you were sixteen . . . or seventeen . . . or eighteen. You believed because your dreams had started running up against the Line like it was a brick wall that didn't have a single crack. And you believed—

most of all—because you had to. You needed to believe that someone could get out of this town, same way you needed to believe that that someone just might be you.

And you held on to that belief. You had to. You held on, and it saw you through the Run, saw you crowned the winner. And it saw you down the black road to a cleared patch of dirt in a cornfield, a spot where Jerry Ricks's Smith & Wesson took all your dreams away.

That's the way it was for you, but it wasn't that way for everyone. If you were a guy like Dan Shepard, you walked a different path. When those three special birthdays ticked by and you came up short, the way Dan did . . . well, you found a way to live with it. You made your peace with your failure. If nothing else, you figured you'd had your chance. You took your cuts at the Line, and you fell short, so you really didn't have anyone to blame but yourself. And, hey, it was a bitter pill to swallow, but at least you knew you took those cuts. At least you tried. And if you didn't catch the brass ring, well, hell, it wasn't the end of the world. It was just the way things turned out . . . it was the way things turned out for damn near everyone you knew.

That's right. If you were like Dan Shepard, you weren't alone. Plenty of other guys had to swallow that pill, and they kept on getting up every morning. So did you, if you were a guy like Dan.

You found a job. You filled up your days. And you filled up your nights, too. On one of them you found yourself with a girl who made you feel a little bit better about the way things were, and pretty soon you found yourself with that girl most every night. And a ring went on her finger, and the two of you carried around a couple of keys that matched the same front door, and at night you both found your way through it and closed that door behind you and, together, you waited for the morning to come.

That's the way it was for you if you weren't a winner. And it wasn't so bad, really. Even when you finally started to figure things out, it wasn't so bad, because you still had each other when that door closed at night, and maybe if you were really lucky you had something else to go along with that, something that was a little bit of both of you, something that allowed you to push away the truth just a little bit longer.

But by the time your first kid was out of diapers, you couldn't run from the truth anymore. You knew about that cornfield. You knew about all those young men buried in that black soil. Once you'd thought those poor bastards had gone somewhere better, when they really hadn't gone anywhere at all. And now you thought about them sleeping down there in the dirt as you stared up at the ceiling in the middle of the night. And you thought about them every time you heard your own boy cry out as he woke from a nightmare in his tiny little bedroom down the hall.

And you told yourself that you really shouldn't worry so much, that the odds are really in his favor. They only took one boy a year. And it wasn't your decision. It wasn't your call. It was only the way it was, and you really didn't have anything to do with it at all. It was those steel-rail bastards in the Harvester's Guild who kept that trainload of misery rolling year after year after year, and no one could stand up to them.

You told yourself that, but it didn't slow your thumping heart. Your fear was there between the pulse beats, no matter what you said. And it banged at you, because, hell, you weren't sixteen, or seventeen, or eighteen anymore. You knew better than to believe the lies that people told you. You knew better than that because you'd learned there were other things besides dreams that could make your heart pound like it was ready to batter its way through your rib cage and take off on its own.

Turned out it didn't matter what you'd learned, because the years swept by regardless. And one day, your boy turned sixteen. And one night, he stepped through your front door. And you let him go, knowing what you knew. And you were there when he hit the finish line, and you were there when he was crowned a winner, and it didn't matter at all that you tried to stop it, because by then there was no way to stop it.

What mattered was that you made it home that night, and your boy didn't. What mattered was that you got up the next morning, and he didn't have the chance. And that's the way it was from there on out—night after night, morning after morning. It turned out the whole deal was really as simple as that.

And now you sit in a church with a shotgun cradled in your arms, staring down at your hands, knowing full well all the things you did with them and all the things you didn't do.

You see the ditches there in your skin, and you can almost hear the shovels working. And you wonder what those hands will do this night, and you wonder how bad they'll ache tomorrow morning.

Outside, young men are screaming in the streets.

You listen to the sound for a few long minutes . . . and then the sound drifts away.

In its place comes a smell that drifts through the open back door.

The raw stink of smoke.

You walk to the front door of the church and open it. Boys are running down Main, toward Oak. A couple miles to the north, flames score the sky.

Sirens scream in the night. A fire truck roars by, and a police cruiser follows. But you don't think of the sirens . . . or the truck or the car . . . or the fire.

You think of your son, beating the hell out of the odds just a year ago.

You think of your son, beating the hell out of the odds tonight.

You feel it, down deep, in your bones. You know he's coming. Your boy. Jim. The son you let down. He's coming here . . . and he's coming soon. You close your eyes and you can see him—the heavy church door creaks open like a castle drawbridge in an old horror movie, and that misshapen thing from the cornfield steps through the gap. You close your eyes and you can see him—a little kid reaches for a doorknob in a tiny three-bedroom house, and that pink-faced baby you once held in your arms steps out into the world on his own for the very first time.

You see all that in your mind's eye. In your mind's eye, you see everything.

The riot gun in your hands weighs about a thousand pounds.

But you manage to lift it.

You manage to lift it one more time.

So that's the way it goes for Dan Shepard. Hey—no surprises there. That's the way the cards hit the table if you live in a town where *winning* is just another name for *losing*.

And that's the way it is for the kind of men who worry about the furrows life has carved in their hands, the kind who happen to be the fathers of sons. Dan Shepard, alone in that church with a cop's shotgun . . . he's one. But there's another man, this one sitting in a chair in a beat-up living room. There's a bottle on the table in front of him, and there's a telephone receiver clutched tightly in his fist.

Jeff McCormick's son is on the other end of that line. Pete's out there somewhere in the darkness. A lot has happened to him since he walked out the door a few hours ago. He's figured out a few things, and he's running on adrenaline and something else—something that crackles through the phone line like electricity.

"So it's all true," Pete says. "Everything I just said. None of it's a lie."

McCormick stares at that bottle on the table. "You've got to understand, Pete. I never had a say in any of this. None of us did. Not me, not my father, not his."

"And not me. I didn't have a say, because no one told me the truth."

"The truth isn't something you get around here. Maybe you understand that now. But I never wanted you hurt. You have to understand that, too."

"But you gave me that machete. You let me walk out that door."

"I did." Pete's father swallows hard after saying those words, staring at that bottle, but he doesn't reach for it. "Everything you said earlier tonight . . . I know why you feel the way you do, but you don't know the whole story. I did some things after your mom died. Stupid things. The drinking was part of it . . . but only part. Things wouldn't have gone so bad if I'd kept it to myself, but I ended up in a bar one night. Jerry Ricks was there, and so was Ralph Jarrett. I was drunk . . . angry . . . I started talking about the town, about the way we all lived. I said I'd lost your mom to cancer, but I wasn't going to lose you to the Run—"

"More words."

"Maybe you're right. If I hadn't been drunk, I probably wouldn't have had the guts to say anything at all. But I did, and it cost me. When I went to work the next morning, Joe Grant called me into the office and canned me. He didn't even tell me why. He didn't have to."

"Right then, we should have loaded up the car. We should have gotten the hell out of here."

"No . . . losing my job was just the tip of the iceberg. Guys like Ricks and Jarrett play a lot harder than that with anyone who gives them a reason. Taking my paycheck was their way of teaching me a lesson. They wanted to pin me in a corner, like everyone else. If we would have run, they would have killed us."

"They'll kill us anyway. I'm not going to spend the next twenty years dying inch by inch, the way you have. If Ricks and his buddies finish me, fine. But I'll go out standing on my feet."

"Will you, Pete? Really? Do you really think it's that easy to die? If it meant taking someone else with you . . . if it meant taking Kim—"

No. Jeff McCormick bites off those words. The conversation's spinning out of control just like it did that night in the bar, and he's as angry as Pete is now, but his fight isn't with his son. It's with Ricks, and Jarrett, and every other guy in the Harvester's Guild.

His entire adult life, Jeff's known this town's dirty little secret. He knew it tonight when his son stepped through the door, but knowing didn't make any difference. The Run rolled around the year of his boy's sixteenth birthday, and Jeff McCormick might as well have said: *Sure thing, I'll ante up. I'll toss my only son out there on the green felt. If those are the rules of the game, that's the way I'll play it.* And it doesn't matter that he wanted to stop Pete on his way out that door, because when push came to shove he let his boy go, just like everyone else in this damn town. That's what it comes down to—what he *did* . . . not what he *wanted* to do. And that's the reason Jeff McCormick can't say those other words . . . the ones you'd expect. *I'm sorry. I didn't mean it. I'd take it all back if I could.* Those words can never be enough once you've gambled with your own flesh and blood.

So Jeff holds on to his silence. He doesn't have another choice. Not if he wants to hold on to his last shred of self-respect, too. And Pete listens to that silence. He listens, but he still doesn't understand.

"I think we're done now," he says. "I didn't call to argue, anyway. I just wanted you to know that I'm getting out of here tonight. There's a fire burning on the north side. It'll keep everyone around here pretty busy for a while. I can use it as a way out, and I'm going to take it."

"You won't make it, son. Ricks . . . Jarrett . . . those other bastards, they'll stop you any way they know how—"

"Maybe they will, maybe they won't. But I have to try. You can help me, or you can hang up the phone. It's your choice."

Jeff McCormick closes his eyes. He knows his son. He knows what it means for him to ask for help in this moment, thinking what he must think. And the true hell of it is that he can't blame his son for feeling that way. He really can't blame him at all.

But maybe he still has a chance to change that. Maybe it's not too late—

"What do you need, Pete?"

"Like I told you, the fire's on the north side. Grain elevator's on the south. I'm going to get hold of a car, and I'll be there as soon as I can. I want you to bring Kim to me. Pack her stuff. I won't leave without her."

Jeff McCormick's heart sinks. He knows he should say something. He has to say something. But he doesn't have the words—

"It's the right thing, Dad. She'll be better off with me. You know that as much as I do. This time, I need you to deliver. If you don't, I'll come after Kimmy myself."

Just like that, the phone line goes dead. Pete's father cradles the receiver. He opens his eyes. Of course he does. What else can he do? And he's still in the same beat-up living room, and there's still a bottle on the table in front of him.

But there are no second chances.

His boy is gone. Out the door for good.

That door didn't slam a few hours ago.

But it sure slammed now.

Pete hangs up the phone in the theater office.

"If he doesn't come through . . . " Pete says. "If he lets me down one more time . . . "

"He'll come through," Kelly says. "He's got to want what's best for your sister as much as you do. You have to give him that much."

Pete nods, but he can't even trust that simple motion. Kelly's sitting across the desk, staring straight into his eyes. In that moment Pete has nowhere to hide. His head is full of words, but he can't find a way to say a single one of them. And suddenly Kelly looks away, just as he did when he pulled her off of Riley Blake and glimpsed that wildfire running deep and strong in her own eyes, the one he knew he shouldn't see until she wanted him to.

"Hey," he says, reaching across the desk and taking her hand. "It's okay. Really."

And it is. Because there's nothing left inside him that he wants to hide. Not from her.

Kelly raises her head. Their eyes meet again. This time, she doesn't look away.

They don't say anything for a long time.

"Okay?" he asks finally, because now there are tears in her eyes.

"Okay," she says, and then she smiles.

A strong squeeze, and their hands part.

Kelly takes the brakeman's club off the desk.

Pete picks up the .45.

He says, "Let's get the hell out of here."

The big Dodge jumps the tracks—chassis coming down hard, shocks crunching—and Jerry Ricks's teeth clack together so hard that he nearly bites his cigarette in half.

Shit. That's all Ricks needs. He slams the gas pedal with a steel-toed boot and flicks on the high beams. The patrol car speeds through a bright tunnel carved by the headlights, past the market where Ricks gunned down those kids an hour and change ago.

He's heading north, toward the fire.

Make that *fires*. Because dispatch had it wrong. The radio call Ricks caught a couple minutes after parting company with Dan Shepard mentioned one fire, but Jerry spots two towers of flame rising from the north side.

Those fires look to be several blocks apart.

The town has exactly one fire truck.

Shit. Everything's gone nuts tonight. First the deal at the market, now this. If Ricks gets his hands on the pimply-faced arsonist who pulled this crazy stunt, what that kid gets won't be as easy as a bullet. He'll hang him from a tree like a heavy bag and do the job right . . . and slow.

Ricks heads toward the blaze that wasn't called in. He gets on the radio and takes care of that little detail, even though he knows it's pointless. Even the lazy bitch at dispatch is smart enough to figure out that a fire crew can't be two places at once, so guess who gets to pick up the slack—your pal and mine, Jerry Ricks, who's suddenly pretty sure that several city blocks are going to end up as cinders tonight.

All Ricks can do is jump on the problem, maybe contain the blaze if the people who live closest to it aren't already panicking. And if they are, well . . . maybe he can save the asses of the ones that matter before they get barbequed. The way Jerry figures it, there won't be too many of those—the only good news he's got right now is that there aren't many Guild members living in this dumpy little corner of town.

And that's not much if you're looking for a silver lining. Ricks signs off the radio, clips the mic on the dash, and swerves just in time to miss a couple of knotheads running toward the scene. Jesus. As he makes the next couple blocks he notices that there are dozens of kids on the streets, and they're all heading toward the fires . . . every single one of them.

And that's when it hits him.

The identity of the firebug.

Gotta be the October Boy himself, a.k.a. little Jimmy Shepard.

Yeah. Ricks slams his palm against the steering wheel, figuring it all out just that fast. Ol' Hacksaw Face did the deed. Sure he did. And every chuckleheaded kid running on a five-day hunger has fallen for his feint. Because that's what this action is. The freak has them kissing up to the flames like a bunch of idiot moths. He needs a diversion. He had to come up with some way to draw the gangs away from Main Street so he could clear a path to the church, and it looks like he's done just that, because every starving little moron running around in a pair of tennis shoes tonight is beating a path in the wrong direction.

"Well, fuck me with a fistful of splinters," Ricks says. "This boy is good."

Houses blur by on both sides of the patrol car. Flickering pumpkins leer at Ricks from porches, and he can almost hear them laugh. Almost. Because imagination only goes so far with Jerry Ricks. It might crawl up on his shoulder and say *howdy* now and then, but it's never long before he gives it the back of his hand.

And that happens right about now. Ricks stares straight ahead at the blaze silhouetted by peaked rooftops. He butts out the cig he nearly bit in half when the Dodge rattled across the tracks, gets another one started with his Zippo. There's part of him that's thinking maybe it's not too late to stop the fire. But there's another part that wants to forget the whole deal, rip a U-bender and point the Dodge in the other direction, because a glance at his wristwatch tells him that it's 11:30. That leaves Dan Shepard's misfit son thirty solid minutes to make it to the church, and Ricks doesn't trust Dan to do the Guild's dirty work if his kid manages to make it all the way to the finish line before the bell tolls midnight.

But what the hell can he do? Could be the Boy is still up ahead somewhere. That's where the smoke is . . . that's where the fire is . . . maybe that's where his scarecrow ass is, too.

"Goddammit!" Ricks shouts. "Goddammit!"

His foot jams the brakes. He skids to a stop. He's so damn close now. Flames are licking the rooftops just a block away. A half dozen boys race past him, heading for the show with bats and pickaxes and chains. The idiots don't even realize that no one's coming to fight the fires besides good old Officer Ricks. They don't even know how close they are to running headfirst into a blast furnace they'll never escape.

Ricks sits there behind the wheel, just sits there like he never has before in his life. For the first time he can remember, he can't make a decision, and he can't fucking stand it. He drags so hard on his cigarette that he nearly burns it down to the filter. And then a kid comes running toward him. A big kid. Ricks thinks he remembers him . . . maybe from the football team. Yeah. The kid looks familiar. But his face is swollen, and his nose looks like it ate fifteen rounds' worth of jabs. Someone must have bashed him good . . . and more than once.

He's pounding on Ricks's window, screaming something. Jerry grabs his .38 with one hand, rolls the window down with the other. The kid stumbles back when he sees the gun.

"Christ . . . no! Don't shoot!"

"Calm down. What the hell do you want?"

"I saw Sawtooth Jack! He's a couple blocks over . . . in front of the Bagley place. He had the gas cap off Old Man Bagley's pickup, and he was stuffing a rag into it—"

And then it's like someone shook up the whole damn world and popped the cap. *Boom!* The sound sucks any words the kid had left in him right out of his mouth, and the concussion nearly knocks him flat-ass on the blacktop.

But Ricks barely notices. He's too busy watching a fireball climb the ladder of the night like a demon laying siege to Heaven. He's watching that fire paint the sky, and everything beneath it—the silent houses, the hard cold streets, the white hood of his patrol car.

Something plows through the orange glow. Two dead-white headlights spear Ricks's retinas. He squints but doesn't look away as a car burns by. Maybe it's a Chevy . . . or a Chrysler. . . .

"Jesus Christ—it's him!" the kid shouts. "It's the October Boy! He boosted Mitch Crenshaw's ride!"

Ricks eyeballs the rearview as the Chrysler's taillights swim away in the murk. The driver's making tracks, heading downtown . . . where there's probably not a kid in sight anymore . . . where the only thing to stop him is a used-up crybaby with a riot gun.

Ricks knows he can't count on that.

He looks at his watch. It's twenty-five minutes to midnight.

He shoots a glance at the swollen-faced kid that is all business.

"Get in," he says. "Now."

The kid's jaw drops open, but no words come out. He runs around to the shotgun side of the patrol car, fills the space with his sizable ass and slams the door. Ricks peels out just that fast, trailing those taillights swimming away in the dark.

Between that Chrysler and the pair of hands strangling the patrol car's steering wheel, Ricks's reflection floats on the windshield—his narrow face painted in dashboard green glow, the tip of his cigarette glowing like a fuse. Ricks glances over at the kid. The big dope doesn't look like a winner. If he's got anything in common with the other young bucks who ended up in that cornfield with a couple ounces of lead ricocheting around in their brainpans, he's doing a pretty solid job of hiding it.

But the way things are turning out, he'll have to do.

"I don't have time to draw you a diagram," Ricks says.

Then he tosses his pistol into the kid's lap.

The October Boy is just about to cross the railroad tracks when something rams the Chrysler's rear bumper.

The Boy glances in the rearview but doesn't see a thing. Just as he realizes his pursuer must be running dark, a pair of high beams scald him from behind. Top that off with a screaming siren and a big ripe cherry that blooms on top of the car that's tail-grabbing his ass, and the Boy finally gets a clue.

The prowl car rams him again, and Jim Shepard's pumpkin head whiplashes on his braided-vine neck like it's ready to come off. Gotta be Jerry Ricks on his backside. Only that crazy bastard would pull a stunt like this.

The Boy mashes the gas pedal. The Chrysler rockets forward, but the police cruiser stays right there with him—the space between the two cars isn't even as wide as a coffin. Both cars pass beneath a streetlight and the Boy catches a quick glimpse of Ricks. For a second the cop is boxed up in the confines of the Chrysler's rearview, his forehead creased above a cold pair of eyes, a cigarette pinched between his lips, the tip of that cig glowing like he's sucking on a red-hot coal—

Bam! Another jolt. The Boy grapples with the wheel and pulls the Chrysler out of a skid, but it's hard to do the job when your hands are only a collection of vines. Still, he manages it, and his foot is hard on the gas like those severed tangles have grown around the pedal and set root in the floorboards. We're talking *planted*.

Another glance in the rearview. Another streetlight illuminates the prowl car's interior. Ricks is smiling now. He's not alone in the car. For the first time the Boy notices that the cop has a passenger, a kid who's leaning out the window—

Three quick flashes from behind. Three hard pops sound in the night, but the October Boy doesn't hear them. He only hears the sound of shattering glass as the Chrysler's rear window explodes. Bullets scream through the cab. One rips through the Boy's shoulder, another trenches the rind of his face, and the third doesn't hit anything but the front windshield . . . which shatters like a wall of ice.

Chunks of glass splatter Jim Shepard's freakshow hands. He whips the wheel to the side as two more shots ring out, and he doesn't even have time to wonder where the bullets went. Main Street is only a couple blocks ahead. A hard right turn and another hundred yards beyond that . . . well, that's where you'll find the old brick church.

He's almost there.

The cold night wind blasts through the broken window. It whips around the cab, nearly snuffing the autumn fire in the Boy's carved head, but he won't let that happen. No way. Not now. He's really hauling ass. Going seventy. He knows he's only got one chance. He's got to punch the brakes just right, then hang on through the turn, and—

Now. He's got to do it *now*.

Jim's knotted foot jams the brake. He whips the steering wheel to the right just as Ricks jackhammers the Chrysler's rear bumper one last time. The steering wheel whipsaws out of the Boy's hands, yanking off a couple of his fingers as if they were ripe carrots. The wheel spins left as the two cars part and the Chrysler's rear bumper tears loose, sparking against the blacktop, disappearing beneath the tires of the prowl car like a gleaming switchblade driven into the belly of a two-tone cat.

The front tires blow. The bumper chews undercarriage. Jerry Ricks tears at the steering wheel, because somehow a streetlamp has ended up in the middle of the road and it looks like there's a brick wall behind it . . . and if you had time for a little Q&A session, the October Boy would surely tell you that a streetlamp and a brick wall sound like a pretty sweet deal to him, because the Chrysler's not on four wheels anymore. No. It's on two . . . until the road slams the driver's side door, and the side window blows out, and the hardtop screams as the Chrysler goes ass over teakettle while the laws of physics grind their heels into the October Boy's best-laid plans—

A couple ticks of the second hand, and two cars are totaled.

It's quiet for twenty seconds. Maybe thirty.

In that time, Jim Shepard's buried in a dark place, like a seed planted too deep in the ground. It's not a new sensation. In fact, it's much too familiar. For Jim remembers the cornfield . . . and Jerry Ricks's pistol against his head . . . and the sound of shovels filling his grave with hard black earth.

So he fights through the darkness, battling for clarity the same way a green tendril tunnels through earth to find the sun. The shadows disappear for a second, and then they're back. A flash of October light, and then another, and Jim sees his carved features projected on the black upholstery a few feet from his face.

Jim reaches for that reverse silhouette with a right hand that's short two fingers, but his arm gives up and his hand slaps against his chest like a fistful of chaff. The Chrysler's upside down. Jim's flat on his back against the hardtop. An electric sizzle pulses in his head, projecting flickering light on that upholstery above—Jim's smile and eyes wink out in time to the sizzle, his arrowhead gash of a nose blinking like a bad bulb in a string of party lights.

Jim can't do much more than lie there. His eyes wink in, wink out. His smile comes and goes. And there's a new feature, one he can chalk up to the accident—a jagged crack running from the stem at the top of his head, through his right eye, into one corner of his grin. The wound flashes like a lightning bolt against the upholstery. Again . . . and again . . . and again. . . .

And it stabs Jim now. The next flash bucks through his body as the crack strobes on the seat above. His body spasms again, as if his muscles were corded with stripped electrical wire rather than pumpkin vine and someone just plugged him into a live socket. Jesus. He feels like some old movie monster—like Frankenstein riding the lightning one more time . . . only it's not working the way it's supposed to . . . the juice is burning him up instead of firing his battery.

Jolt. Jim's right hand flaps against his chest like a hooked fish.

Jolt. Candy wrappers rustle inside him like wastepaper balled up in a giant fist.

Jolt. Jim tries to roll over. God, he wishes he could roll over. But he can't even seem to move his hand now. It's there on his chest, glued to a hole carved in his shoulder by one of the kid's bullets, a hole that's leaking sticky nougat and marshmallow cream all over his denim jacket.

Jolt.

The head crack sparks.

Jolt.

The lightning sizzles.

Jolt.

Another spasm wracks the October Boy's body.

Ricks manages to get his eyes open. Pretty quickly he wishes he hadn't, because his reflection's waiting there on the windshield. Blood's dripping from a gash in his forehead, and his left cheek's carved like someone got his holidays mixed up and mistook Ricks's face for a Thanksgiving turkey. But it's that leaky forehead that bothers Jerry the most. Blood's spilling over his brow, splattering his eyelids. Hell, he feels like someone doused his eyeballs with a handful of salt.

The cop wipes blood and sweat out of his eyes—he's sweating like a goddamn mule. He blinks a few times. Things come a little clearer. The streetlamp's nowhere in view—he must have missed that—but he spots that brick wall easy enough. He didn't make out so hot with that. Spun the Dodge sideways, caved in the left side of the front end coming up against it, and the rest of the driver's side ended up kissing those bricks pretty good. He could stick his tongue out the window and lick the damn things if he wanted to. No way he's getting out the driver's side of the patrol car now. Even with the side window broken, he doesn't have the room to crawl out.

Not that he could, the way he's feeling. Cut up, cracked up, his body hammered straight through. As for his face, must be that the glass sliced him up when the side window broke. Could even be that his head did the job on the window.

Things start to swim as he tries to remember. It's weird. He's trying to recall the accident, when he knows he should be thinking of something else . . . something that's important. . . .

Ricks blinks again. Kicks his own ass out of dreamland.

Yeah. There's the world. The one he needs to grab hold of. It's clear . . . and sharp—

"Are you all right?" the kid says.

Jesus. Ricks forgot the kid was there. Apart from his busted-up nose—which the kid had before the accident— he looks all right. He's even got Ricks's pistol in his hand and—

The October Boy, Ricks thinks. Sure. That's the important thing he couldn't quite remember. *Where's the goddamn Boy?*

He looks to the road. The Chrysler never made that turn onto Main. It's upside down, bashed in, finished. Ricks reaches across the kid, gets the glove compartment open. It feels like his head is going to roll off his shoulders when he does that. As he grabs a box of cartridges, he's praying that the Boy isn't as *finished* as that fucking Chrysler looks. Because if the Boy's done, and if Ricks's Dodge did the job instead of one of the kid's bullets, then it's all over.

For everything that's penned up in the city limits, anyway.

Finished. Done. End of story.

But maybe it isn't that way. Maybe the Boy's still sucking wind. If that's the deal, then the town—and everyone in it—still stands a chance.

Ricks glances at his watch. It's 11:45. Still plenty of time to get the job done. He spills bullets into his hand. They're out of focus. Blood drips on them from the wounds in his head. For a second it looks like he's got a handful of fresh-spawned trout taking a bath in his blood.

Whoa, boy. Don't go swimming in those waters.

Ricks closes his eyes, shakes his head. He doesn't have time for this addle-brained shit. When he opens his eyes, the fish are gone. The bullets are back. He hands them to the kid, but the moron just sits there, staring at them.

Ricks doesn't bother to look at him. Instead he sits there for a long moment, waiting for the sound of the opening door, hoping the kid will get a clue on his own.

Things get kind of shadowy for a while. Maybe ten seconds. Maybe fifteen.

"If you want to finish this job," Ricks says, "you'd better get your ass moving."

Ricks turns to the kid, just to make sure he got the message.

But the car door is open.

The kid is already gone.

Riley Blake swallows hard.

Man oh man. He never thought he'd win the Run.

He walks down Main Street, the cop's pistol gripped tightly in his hand. Behind him, to the north, the three fires crawling through the poor side of town have become one roaring inferno. But fire isn't Riley's problem. He can't think about it now. There's only one thing on his mind, and it's over there inside Mitch Crenshaw's bashed Chrysler.

Riley hopes that thing isn't dead.

It better not be dead.

Because Riley Blake's got dibs on its homegrown ass. Uh-huh. It's ten minutes to midnight, and the October Boy is all his. There's no one else around. *No competition* . . . and that means *no sweat*. Twenty steps . . . maybe twenty-five . . . and Riley will be right there at that Chrysler.

He keeps walking, loading bullets into Ricks's .38 as he goes. He feeds the pistol six, then slaps the cylinder closed.

He tries to tell himself that the hacked-up bastard back there in the prowl car wouldn't give this job a second thought, but he knows he's nothing like Jerry Ricks.

And he doesn't have to be. Ten minutes is plenty of time to do the job and still be careful about it. And that's probably a very good idea, because Riley knows all about the thing over there in that wreck. Call it the October Boy . . . or Ol' Hacksaw Face . . . or Sawtooth Jack . . . it's a thing that goes by a dozen other names, a monster that can conjure a year's worth of nightmares in a heartbeat.

That's why Riley takes it slow. . . .

That's why Riley takes it easy. . . .

Ten feet away from the wreck, he kneels and peeks inside the cab. Something's moving in there, bucking against the hood of the car like some sadist wired it to the Chrysler's battery. The sight rattles Riley just a little bit, but he steadies his nerve, tells himself that *moving is good*. Moving means the thing is still alive.

Riley raises the pistol and takes aim. Just as he begins to think this is going to be really easy, the thing in the Chrysler rolls over . . .

. . . and drops on its elbows . . .

. . . and starts crawling.

Not fast, but not at all slow, either. As it moves, one of its hands flexes open. Something feeds through the vines of its left wrist, extending into the thing's grasp like a mutant cat's claw. It's a butcher knife, and it gleams in the firelight spilling over Riley's shoulder, and the October Boy's fingers close around it as he raises his carved-up head and stares straight at the boy with the gun.

Jolts of wild lightning jag through the thing's head. It's like watching an electrical storm. Something about it mesmerizes Riley . . . something about the way the light spills through those triangular eyes. He can't seem to look away from it; he can't seem to think. And all the while the pumpkin-headed thing keeps staring at him as it crawls through the busted window, elbowing across the blacktop with that knife in its hand.

And now Riley can smell the monster. Scorched cinnamon, and gunpowder, and melted wax—the stink is all mixed up in the October Boy's fireball of a head, and that head looks like the devil's own stewpot on the boil.

The stink shakes Riley out of his reverie.

He raises the pistol . . . cocks the hammer . . .

And something smashes against his arm. *Hard.* Riley drops the .38. He stumbles, grabbing his right biceps as he manages to turn around. . . .

And there's the girl. That same damn girl. That redhead—

"Miss me?" she asks.

Then she hits him again.

The brakeman's club cracks against Riley's skull.

The next thing he sees is pavement coming up fast.

Pete hauls the October Boy away from the wreck. He's actually glad the Chrysler flipped on its lid. He and Kelly barely dodged it while crossing Main after leaving the movie theater, and that was the third time tonight he was lined up in front of that rolling monster's headlights. He's beginning to think the heap has it in for him. And maybe that isn't a bad idea—because even now the Chrysler isn't completely dead. Its Gorgon headlights are still blazing, and Pete doesn't want to get caught in their glow even if the heap's wheels are pointed skyward.

Pete drags the Boy to the sidewalk. The butcher knife slips out of the Boy's grasp and clatters against the roadway, but the Boy doesn't even notice. It seems like the thing that used to be Jim Shepard doesn't even know what's going on. He makes no resistance as Pete settles him against a mailbox at the curb.

While Pete's doing that, Kelly stares down at Riley Blake, the club cocked and ready if he so much as moves.

He doesn't. He's out cold.

Pete stops for a second, catching his breath. Then he walks toward Riley, shooting Kelly a glance. "You lowered the boom on this guy twice tonight," he says, grabbing the football player's boots and dragging him away from the wrecked car. "I think maybe you enjoyed it a little too much."

"Damn right I did. And I won't lie about it, either."

"Fair enough. You did that job. Now let's do another."

"What are you talking about?"

Pete drops Riley Blake's feet in the gutter and nods in the Boy's direction. "I mean, I don't think our friend here's going to make it anywhere on his own."

"Whatever plan you've got, I hope it's not complicated . . . we have about five minutes between now and midnight."

"We'll keep it simple, then."

Pete bends low, ducks his head under the Boy's right arm, sets him on his feet.

"Okay," Pete says. "Let's get him to the church on time."

Ricks can't believe he hasn't heard a shot yet, and that can only mean one of two things—either the Boy was creamed in the accident, or the dipshit he sent to pull the trigger is dragging ass.

Well, hell, Ricks tells himself. *Maybe it's time for Mother to go hold the little moron's hand.* He slides across the passenger seat and makes it out of the car. Stands up, but nearly doesn't stay up, so he grabs the top of the car door to steady himself.

That's when he sees the goddamn football player over there on the ground, laid out like he's ready for flowers. And there's another kid. Two of them, actually. A boy and a girl, and both of them are on their feet and moving. The boy has Sawtooth Jack slung over his shoulder like a wounded soldier. He's dragging him in the direction of the church while the girl brings up the rear, watching the shadows for trouble.

Ricks can't believe his eyes. He blinks, but it doesn't do any good. Forget bullets that look like trout and all that other screwy horseshit—this is the worst nightmare he can imagine. It doesn't make any sense at all.

"Hey . . . " he shouts. "Hey!"

The girl glances in his direction, but she doesn't slow down at all, and neither does the boy.

Ricks suddenly recognizes both of them.

Jesus! Kelly Haines and Pete McCormick. Just my goddamn luck!

He reaches for his holster . . . and finds it empty.

And why's that, Jerry?

Well . . . maybe it's because you gave your pistol to the kid.

And you gave your riot gun to Dan Shepard.

All you've got is a fucking nightstick.

And it's three minutes to midnight, you stupid sack of shit.

So get your ass moving. . . .

Pete and Kelly don't run. The October Boy can't.
But they move.

Kelly turns her back on Jerry Ricks, and that's a relief. The pissed-off cop looks like he shaved with a cheese grater. He wasn't any picnic before he looked like he'd been skinned alive. She sure doesn't want a piece of him now.

Kelly's still not in top form herself, but she pulls even with Pete.

"You'd better hurry," she says.

Pete's breaths come hard and fast. "Doing the best I can."

And that's what Ricks is doing, too, because the clock is short another half-minute, leaving two and a half until the final bell.

His .38's on the ground by the wrecked Chrysler. Ricks snatches it up. Glances over at the three figures heading toward the church while he does that, and the whole deal's making sense to him now. Ricks doesn't need a round of interrogation to figure out that Haines and McCormick have managed to add two and two together when it comes to figuring out the grand scheme of things . . . and they've managed that feat at the worst possible moment.

See, Jerry's long-barreled Smith & Wesson won't do him any good. He can't fire the pistol. He can't risk taking a shot at McCormick, because he might nail the Boy instead.

And if he blows a hole through Mr. Pumpkinhead, the whole goddamn deal will go straight to hell.

Has to be a kid nails that walking nightmare.

And it has to happen in the next two minutes.

Those are the rules.

Jerry looks around. There's no one in sight.

Except that one damn football player. Flat-assed on his back. Over there in the gutter. . . .

They're halfway up the church stairs when Pete loses his grip on the Boy. As he lurches to the side, Pete makes a grab for his denim jacket and misses. Just when he's ready for the sound of pumpkin splattering against brick staircase, Kelly catches the Boy by his frayed collar.

Together they haul Jim Shepard onto the tangled vines that pass for his feet.

"Okay," Pete says. "I've got him now."

Kelly takes the stairs two by two.

"I hope that door isn't locked," she says.

The kid says, "They're a long way off. I don't know if I can—"

"Shut up and do it," Ricks says. "You've got six shots. Make one of them count."

The kid takes aim.

The bell in the church steeple begins to toll the hour.

"Pull the trigger, idiot! Do it now!"

Three bullets chew at the door just as Kelly throws it open. She ducks inside. Two more shots ring out as Pete and the Boy stumble past her.

Kelly heaves the door shut and sets the lock.

She turns, her eyes searching the darkness.

"Pete?" she asks. "Are you all right?"

There's no answer. It's as if she's speaking to the shadows.

The bell tolls.

For the ninth time . . . the tenth . . . the eleventh. . . .

PART FOUR
Blood

The bell tolls midnight.

Ricks says: "Give me the pistol."

"I think I hit him," Riley says, handing over the .38. "I'm pretty sure that last shot—"

"Uh-uh. You didn't hit shit, kid. Unless you want to count that church door. You hit that thing five fucking times. But don't worry about it. At least you did one thing right."

"What do you mean?"

"You pulled the trigger five times. That means you left one bullet in the gun. And being as it's past midnight, there's one place I'd really like to put it."

"Huh?"

Ricks smiles. Jesus. This kid really is a spud with a pretty thick jacket.

He jams the .38 under Riley Blake's chin.

He pulls the trigger.

Two hundred and thirty pounds of *useless* hits the ground.

Kelly grips Pete's hand in the darkness. "Thank God you're okay. Those last two shots when you were coming through the door—I thought you might have been hit."

"No," Pete says. "I'm still on my feet. Looks like he is, too."

Ahead of them, the October Boy walks slowly down the aisle. He's unsteady but holding on, his left hand catching the endcaps of oak pews as he advances from one row to the next. Ribbons of moonlight spill through narrow stained-glass windows, falling like bars across his path. They're the color of blood and bruises, and the Boy wades through them, his battered head dipping on that braided-vine neck, light from the lightning-bolt crack flashing through the stained murk like a yellow knife.

Pete watches, not quite trusting his own eyes.

It's past midnight, and the October Boy is still on his feet.

It's past midnight, and the October Boy is inside the church.

He's won.

Six hours ago, Pete never could have imagined that he'd be standing in this place, silently celebrating the

Boy's victory. It's a strange moment, because Pete knows he made that victory possible. Just a few hours ago he was intent on killing the thing that's walking down the aisle on scarecrow legs, and now he'd run to help the Boy if he stumbled.

But the October Boy doesn't stumble. He moves forward with head bowed, approaching an icon this town abandoned long ago. Pete stares at the big cross nailed up there on the wall. That thing has never meant much to him. He sat beneath it on a thousand Sunday mornings he can't recall. He sat beneath it on one day—the day of his mother's funeral—that he'll never forget. He knows what the cross is supposed to mean, and there's a part of him that would like to think that maybe it could mean those things—in another place, to other people. But not here, not to him, and not to a boy who ended up on his knees in a cornfield with a gun pressed against his head while an entire town turned its back.

So the sight of the October Boy moving toward the cross—slowly, almost reverently—surprises Pete McCormick. But Jim Shepard's head is bowed no longer. As he nears the altar, he stares up at the cross. His carved features are projected on the wall ahead, and the crack slicing from stem to chin covers the cross like a jagged hunk of molten steel just pulled from a forge.

And then the Boy looks away, and the wall goes black. The light from his head spotlights the floor below the altar. There's something there, something Pete didn't notice until now, something that lies hidden in the darkness.

Pete starts up the aisle, straining to see the thing that separates the Boy from the cross.

The thing the Boy was focused on all along as he walked the aisle with head bowed.

A few steps, and Pete sees that thing clearly.

It's a dead man with a shotgun clutched tightly in his hands.

The gun is aimed at the place where his head used to be.

Ricks doesn't waste time looking at the dead boy lying face down on the blacktop. The fat punk doesn't matter now. The way the lawman sees it, nothing much matters, because it's five minutes past midnight, and the pumpkin-headed freak is inside the church, and that means an entire way of life just went to hell in a handbasket.

Uh-huh. The October Boy ran the fucking gauntlet. He made it down the black road . . . made it all the way through town. Got two tons of Detroit steel wrapped around him and managed to crawl away. Five lead slugs drilled holes in a door as he ducked through it, and not one of them splattered his Jack o' Lantern skull. And once he made it inside the church . . . well, things must have been just fine and dandy in there as the bell tolled twelve, because Ricks sure as hell didn't hear any riot gun booming in the night.

The cop doesn't waste time wondering what happened to Dan Shepard. He doesn't care if the weepy bastard turned rabbit and hippity-hopped down the road; he doesn't care if Shepard's down on his knees kissing his misfit kid's feet. The only thing that matters to Ricks is that the end credits are rolling on the world as he knows it. All you have to do is take a quick glance to the north and you'll see the curtain coming down on this show.

Hell, forget *coming down*. The damn curtain's burning up. Those three fires kindled by the October Boy have joined together into one king-size conflagration that's cremating the poor side of town. It's like someone dumped a bucket of coals on the curtains in the movie theater across the street, and the flames are burning that dark velvet to cinders, scorching the night clean off the raw white screen underneath.

Jesus. That's a hell of a thing to think.

The lawman plucks six cartridges from his gunbelt. This time they don't look anything like a fistful of fresh-spawned trout. He feeds the bullets into the .38's cylinder and starts across Main Street.

He checks his step as a rattletrap Chevy makes the corner of Oak and blows by him, and by the time his foot hits the curb on the other side of the street an old Ford's doing the same. Ricks turns to the west, watching that Chevy blow across the Line, watching the Ford do the same. Both cars cross the city limits just like that . . . like there's no Line at all anymore, and no Jerry Ricks to stop them, and no Harvester's Guild to watch for in the rearview mirror.

Taillights swim in the distance as the two cars disappear into the night. Ricks wipes a trickle of blood from the gash in his forehead. Wow. He steps off the curb on one side of the street, and the world works one way. By the time he makes it to the opposite curb, things don't work that way anymore. That's how fast people change when the status quo goes up in flames. *The hell with this*, they figure, and they get their scorched asses out of Dodge PDQ.

Some people might call that courage. Ricks won't go that far. The way he sees it, the people in those cars are just about as brave as a pack of rats skittering off a sinking ship before it heads for Davey Jones's locker. You want to call that courage—go ahead, that's fine with Jerry. In the end, it doesn't matter what you call it. What matters is that it does the same job—those cars are gone, and the black road waits for more, and Jerry Ricks doesn't figure it will be waiting for long.

Well, he figures, *that's the way the mop flops.* Maybe in a little while, Jerry will get his ass out of Dodge, too. Maybe . . . but first he's got some unfinished business to attend to. He's got six bullets in his gun, and he figures that'll be just enough to batten down the hatches on the way things used to be.

The dead man's face is gone, pale skin butchered to blood and bone by the shotgun still gripped in his hands. Even so, the October Boy recognizes the corpse. He knows this man's hands, and he recognizes the simple gold wedding ring on his finger.

Jim Shepard is the product of that ring. Seeing it now there is only one word in his head, and it's the same word that crossed his bristling smile when his father finished carving his face just a few hours ago.

Why?

Jim's father didn't give his son an answer when Jim spoke that word in the cornfield, but he has given him one now. It's plain enough, lying there on the floor. Mute, voiceless. Skinned of the components that allowed it to see and the part of it that could smile. Stripped down to red meat and the ruined mechanics of bone and muscle.

That's the way you look once you're broken for good. If you're a man, not a machine, and your gears are stripped smooth and you just can't run anymore. And that's what the men in the Guild didn't understand when they placed Dan Shepard between the finish line and his eldest son. They put Dan there to stop his boy, when they should have realized that his gearbox had been ground down to filings a year ago, out in that cornfield. He could never haul that load again. Pop the hood, check the engine, you'll see that clearly. Take the machine down to muscle and bone, test the wear and tear on the life contained in that wedding ring and the easy trigger action on that shotgun, you'll wonder how anyone could have figured Dan was capable of stopping anyone besides himself.

Hell, a kid who just spent a year buried in the ground can see that plain enough, and he just has a couple of holes hacked in his hollow head—he doesn't even have any eyes.

"You figuring it out yet, you fucking freak?" Jerry Ricks screams from the street. *"You king of the hill now? You cock of the walk? Uh-uh. You know better than that, don't you? You're just a goddamn weed with a heartbeat. That's all you were when you came out of the ground, and it's all you'll be from here on out. 'Cause you've got nowhere else to go!*

"Yeah!" Ricks yells. *"Twelve dings of a bell didn't really change much, did it, Jimmy? You should have let one of those wet-nosed morons take you down when you had a chance! They would have done it quick! Not me, boy . . . I'm gonna make sure you suffer! I'm gonna prune you back an inch at a time!"*

Staring down at the broken remains of his father, those words gust through Jim's head like a winter wind. But words can't extinguish the fire that burns there. Jim's sawtoothed smile closes in a tight grimace as he takes his father's hand in his own. Gently, he slides the wedding ring from Dan Shepard's finger. He holds it there in his wounded hand—the hand with three fingers—for a long moment.

"I'll take care of the rest of you, too!" Ricks screams. *"Don't think I won't! Every one of you in there is as good as dead! McCormick . . . Kelly Haines. And if you're in there, Dan, I'm coming for you, too, you sniveling piece of shit!"*

Oh, yes. Dan is here, along with all those other fathers who ended up in that cornfield, and all those other sons who died while their fathers watched. Jim feels his father in the ring he holds in his hand. He feels the others in the places where rusty nails punctured his knotted body and held him to a crosspiece.

He feels all of them. Here. Now.

Those feelings linger, but Jim Shepard does not. He slides that band of gold onto the ring finger of his left hand. In another moment he's on his feet. He turns his back to the altar, his carved eyes trained on the young man standing near the church door.

The October Boy starts toward him.

The fury in his eyes lights up the shadows.

His sandpaper voice scrapes over the pews.

"Give me your gun," he says.

Spoken in the October Boy's voice, those words can only sound like a threat. They strip a layer off Pete's bravery. His fear is a product of the town, the same way the Run is. It's the kind of reaction designed to shatter the bond shared by a couple of boys named McCormick and Shepard. And you understand that better than anyone, because you've walked in Pete McCormick's shoes, and you've walked on the October Boy's severed-root feet. You know them both, and a hundred others like them buried out in that black field where your bones were sown.

So you know what happens in the moment when these two forces converge. That moment has always been the same, as inevitable as it is explosive. But that's not the way it turned out tonight. Tonight the template changed. One half of that equation reached out to the other, and together they stepped past midnight into a moment where everything was different.

That moment passes between them now, in a single glance. The scorching glare from a pair of carved sockets reveals the icy gleam in a pair of blue eyes. Different forms of the same fire, and both are burning bright.

But only one of them can deliver that fire into tomorrow.

For that to happen, the other must burn it down to cinders tonight.

"You can't do it alone," Pete says, because he doesn't want to believe the inevitable. But Jim Shepard knows better. The thoughts contained behind his battered Halloween mask of a face are clear in a way Pete's thoughts can't be.

"I know what's left for me," Jim says.

He looks at Pete, and at the girl, and at the open door behind them.

"The rest is left for you."

Even before the words are spoken, Pete understands what the Boy is saying. A dozen arguments fill his thoughts. But they're his thoughts, not the thoughts he shares with the

Boy, not products of the final night that joins them. And as soon as Pete realizes that, the fire from the Boy's eyes burns every one of Pete's arguments to ashes.

Pete swallows hard and hands over the gun.

There are no other good-byes.

There don't need to be.

Three fingers and a thumb tighten around the butt of the pistol, and the October Boy's index finger creeps through the trigger guard. The boy and the girl hurry down the aisle, heading for the back exit of the church. The Boy's gaze follows them—all hard strobes and flickers, that busted gash spotlighting their path as they make their way through the shadows.

Jim Shepard doesn't want to miss this moment.

It's the one moment tonight that matters most.

Pete McCormick and Kelly Haines pass the altar without a second glance.

The back door stands open, and they step through it together.

The door swings closed.

And the fire inside the October Boy is fed. It's doubly strong now, and it glows brighter than before. Because the boy destined to follow Jim into a cornfield grave is gone. He's headed for the black road, heading toward tomorrow without a detour in sight. And so that fire's eating at that battered rind, warping that lead-lined door that held back an Atomic Fireball fury. It seeps through that jagged crack of a wound, bubbling over those jagged teeth like lava escaping a volcano. It spills down the Boy's neck, following the veins that root inside him, and it drips onto his coat, splashing against frayed blue denim and traveling on, splattering the church floor, scorching black circles on the carpet as the October Boy stalks toward the heavy oaken doors.

"C'mon out of there, chickenshit! Come on out before I come in and—"

Jerry Ricks stands at the bottom of the brick staircase. Gun out, mouth open. Neither does him any good. Because the church doors fly open as that last word crosses his lips, and the October Boy is through the gap before those doors even have a chance to bang against scar-colored bricks.

His head spits fire.

A stolen .45 rises in his hand.

The hammer crashes against hard steel. Muzzle-flash lightning escapes the barrel. A bullet tears through Ricks's shoulder, but he doesn't even feel it. He's too busy pulling the .38's trigger. The slug rips through denim and vine, and the October Boy staggers against the railing as a second and third slug chew holes through his chest.

But he doesn't fall back. Hell, no. He comes forward, fingers closing over the railing as he rides it . . . spilling down those stairs like a two-legged nightmare . . . raising the .45 while he makes the trip. . . .

And another bullet hits Ricks where the first one did, carving the meat off his shoulder. Ricks tries to raise his gun, but the muscles meant to do that job don't work anymore. The pain comes hard and fast, and so does the Boy. He's still charging forward . . . and Ricks stumbles back a half dozen steps . . . and a third bullet chews through his shoulder, chopping his deltoid to hamburger, shearing rotator cuff, shattering his humerus bone in its socket.

Ricks spits his cigarette into the flowerbed lining the brick walkway. His shoulder is jelly hanging off the bone. Convulsively, his finger jerks the .38's trigger one last time, but he's not aiming at anything anymore. The bullet sparks off the brick walkway. The October Boy's whiskbroom foot covers the spot as he advances, firing again. The bullet cores Ricks's guts, exploding a pair of vertebrae on its way out, and Ricks drops his pistol and sinks to his knees.

And there he is. Right there. The Boy is on him now. A cloud of gunpowder . . . the stink of scorched cinnamon. Ricks tastes it in the air, tastes it along with his own blood.

Brown eyes gleam in his skinned face as he stares up at Dan Shepard's kid. The thing from the cornfield doesn't have any eyes. Just a headful of fire. The creature reaches out, fingers twining through Ricks's hair like a trio of rattlesnakes.

It raises the lawman's head; it stares down. Drops of blazing pulp pour over its barbed teeth, splattering Ricks's face like battery acid.

That's bad, but what's coming is worse.

The Boy jams the .45's barrel against Jerry Ricks's temple.

The hot metal scores the lawman's flesh like a branding iron.

A sawtoothed smile lights up the cop's bloody face.

"You remember this part, don't you?"

Those words hit Ricks like another bullet. He glares up at the pumpkin-headed freak. He remembers, all right. Goddamn right he does. Out there in the cornfield. A dozen trips . . . maybe more. A dozen bullets. Maybe more. His gun pressed against all those heads . . . his callused finger pulling the trigger time and time again.

Someone else pulls the trigger now.

Muzzle flash scorches the side of the lawman's head.

Brain and bone and blood splatter the flowerbed.

By the time he hits the ground, Jerry Ricks can't remember anything anymore.

But some things can't be forgotten. Neither can they be contained . . . not within the head of the October Boy, and not within the borders of the dark little town.

Gouts of fire spill through the October Boy's eyes and blacken the wound slashing across his face. He steps over Jerry Ricks's corpse, knowing he has done the last thing this night demands of him, but the fury required to do that thing can't be tamped down now that it has been unleashed.

And so it burns. The October Boy's body is tinder ready for the spark, but his head is a furnace. And the fire in his brain takes things from him—his anger, his pain—but these are not the things he wanted to keep. Those things have passed to another now, and Pete McCormick will carry them with him as he follows a path traveling out of the darkness.

That path, too, is carved by fire. An inferno has ravaged the neighborhoods. Jerry Ricks's house is gone—his gun cabinet is less than a cinder. The heavy bag that hung in his backyard has shed its canvas skin, spilling sand over the black concrete below. The front lawn where Kelly and Pete had their dustup with Riley Blake and Marty Weston is an ashy blanket woven with dying sparks. The market on Oak is a charred carcass, home to flame, swirling soot, and the stink of burning meat.

The air is heavy with smoke. Slivers of black ash skitter across the full moon like bats on the wing, and sparks rain down from the night sky in firefly swarms. They make cradles of dying leaves, catching fire in the oak tree above the October Boy's head, peppering his shoulders with cinder and ash as he follows the brick walkway.

He makes his way to the street. A hot red wave rises above the rooftops across Main. Flames gutter through the alley that parallels the railroad tracks, firing masoned bricks as if they were the walls of a gigantic oven. Blistering heat cracks the weakest bricks like old bones, scorching the inside walls of those buildings, tindering new blazes that burst alive in dark corners. And soon mushrooms of black smoke billow against a dozen ceilings, and hungry flames search for air and fuel—riding lacquered wood, torching cloth and paper, boiling water trapped in pipes, scalding gas lines that rupture and ignite.

Across the street, the movie theater's windows explode. Broken glass rains down, splattering the windshields of two cars racing down Main toward the black road, and a gigantic fireball rolls over the blacktop, singeing their rear bumpers as they pass.

Snakes of fire crawl up the front of the theater, slithering across the marquee, melting the red letters that cling there. The October Boy watches as red plastic drizzles to the cement below. The words slip away; a curtain of sparks rains down. And it's the same inside the Boy. The Red Vines braided within his body melt like the letters on the marquee; pockets of memory burn to black in his head; molten fire peels away wax paper and scorches his beating candy heart.

That's all that is left. Fire in the building, fire in the Boy. Those marquee letters are gone now, and so are his memories. And so are the words and the world they made. Inside the theater, reels of film burn like rolls of midnight crepe. The projectors are melted wrecks. All that remains is a building shorn of purpose, an inferno blazing inside its open brick jaws. And so the October Boy moves toward it with a black skull tottering on his shoulders that looks almost human now, and a jacket that's more ash than denim, and a gun still gripped in his hand.

He walks toward that fiery mouth, smiling his last smile.

This is the place he's meant to go.

This is the place where stories find their endings.

But they don't always die. No. Like fire, like fury, stories can't always be contained.

A car races toward the Boy as he steps into the street. Its windows are glowing orange, as if the car is stoked with coals. There's a face behind that reflected fire, a face that grows smaller as the car whips by. It's a boy's face . . . a little kid staring through the rear window at the burning thing walking in the streets . . . and the boy sheds his blazing mask as the car speeds down Main and the reflection streams off the glass, but he doesn't shed the look of wonder kindled in his eyes.

"The October Boy," he whispers.

The October Boy. . . .

That car speeds away, disappearing into the night. Other cars do the same as the town empties out. Some take the black road, some take roads that head in other directions. But it's not destination that governs the routes they follow. It's raw chance, and rawer emotion—fear and excitement, joy and rage—a thousand different shades smeared across the burning palate of the night.

And that's a different state of affairs around here. In this town the human animal's most unpredictable quality has always been contained, buttoned down, nailed up. Until tonight. Tonight all bets are off. The Harvester's Guild and the men who ran it have scattered in the darkness. The walls are falling in those cramped little houses. The invisible Line that penned up this world is gone.

Pete McCormick understands that as he and Kelly stand at the side of the year-old Cadillac he boosted behind the brick church. Not that it was hard to snatch those wheels—the keys were in the ignition and the gleaming machine's doors were unlocked, just as Pete knew they'd be. Because the man who drove that car was finished with it before he slammed its door for the last time. Pete sees that now, even though he didn't know the man who drove this car. He sees it, because there's a part of him that's looking at things through a pair of carved eyes that belonged to somebody else.

Seen that way, the world looks a little different. So does this moment. It's not the way Pete expected it to look a couple of hours ago, not at all the way he imagined it in his mind's eye. He looks across the gravel parking lot in front of the grain elevator, and there's ample evidence of that. Because, hey, Pete's human, the same way Jim Shepard was.

He's got his own emotional palate, and even now the big brush of the night's working the colors inside him.

Pete feels that happening as his little sister rushes toward him, tears in her eyes.

He feels it, too, as he stares at his father standing there next to his old beater of a Dodge, his lined face headstone gray as he watches his daughter go.

Smoke and ash paint the distance between father and son, but that doesn't hide anything from Pete. His eyes are icy blue, fashioned from flesh and blood that burn and sting in the hot winds whipped by the inferno a couple miles distant, but those aren't the eyes he's looking through now. No. His eyes are a pair of fiery triangles that cut through the smoke and cut through the night. They slice it up the same way they cleaved the darkness that blanketed the brick church, only this time they don't find a dead man on the floor.

No. Not this time.

Kim's feet crunch over gravel as she runs toward her brother. There's a grocery bag clutched in her hands. In a town where no one owns a suitcase, that paper bag's the best she could do. It can't hold much—a few clothes, and a stuffed animal her mother gave her. Not everything Kim wanted to take with her. Not everything she can't do without, or won't miss.

But that's the way it is.

A time like this . . . things the way they are . . . you can't take everything with you.

So you take the things that are most important.

You take the things that can't be left behind.

And that's what Pete McCormick does. His foot's heavy on the gas. The Cadillac burrows through the flames as it speeds down backstreets, catching Main at the edge of town. A quick turn and there's the black road—fire threshing through the corn as the rolling inferno busts the city limits, the Cadillac pressing on through the night as it does the same.

That road does not meander. Like a planned path of escape, it cleaves a sea of blazing quarter sections, and so does the Caddy. The black car races through fields where scores of dead boys lie buried under cornstalk pyres, its big engine fighting for ground as fire climbs a rough-hewn crossbar heavy with rusty nails and tumbles on in the night.

Spark and ash spatter the windshield, but ahead there's hard clean darkness.

Pete charges toward it. Racing the fire, racing the night.

A quick glance in the rearview, and he says, "Look behind you, Dad."

"No," his father says. "Not anymore. Not ever."

Jeff McCormick's eyes are trained on that hard yellow line ahead. He won't look back. But Pete looks, and longer this time. Kim's in the backseat—his little sister is burrowed in Kelly's arms. And behind them the sky is as red as the devil's own furnace, banked tight against a scorched penny of a moon.

The Caddy travels on as that penny melts in the night.

The flames travel, too.

But they can't catch Pete McCormick.

He's much too fast.

He's already gone. . . .

Afterword

You know the stories.

Horror stories, I mean.

After all, you've read enough of them.

But reading probably wasn't the first way you found them. No. Most likely, your first horror stories were spoken, not written. They built toward climaxes that were hard to forget, and they managed to tie knots in your brain with little more than a whisper. To be honest, it's hard for words on a page to compete with that kind of experience. After all, ten-point type can't whisper . . . especially in the dark.

But those first stories could. They were short and sharp and filled with hook-handed killers and buried golden arms, spectral weeping women and vanishing hitchhikers, and the occasional bloody footprint on a staircase in an abandoned house. Maybe you heard them back in the day just as midnight rolled around, told by a brother or sister in a shared bedroom. Or maybe you went down a rabbit hole on YouTube when you got your first laptop, listening to one creepypasta after another until you were sure that *nope, uh-uh, not getting any sleep tonight.*[1]

But how and when you found the good stuff doesn't really matter, as long as those stories did the job. And me? Well, I was lucky. My dad was a great storyteller, and he didn't save the scary ones for nights spent around a campfire out in the woods. Mostly I remember hearing them on summer nights after barbecues in our backyard, the neighborhood dads trading stories as the coals burned down.

I grew up in Vallejo, a blue-collar town north of San Francisco. Almost every dad in our neighborhood worked at Mare Island Naval Shipyard (my dad, a truck driver, was an exception). They'd come from all over—not just the States, but the world—most of them starting families in California after World War II. Lucky for me, they brought their stories with them. So not only did I learn about the mysterious Green Man who was said to roam the streets in my dad's Pennsylvania hometown, I also heard about headless boogeymen who live under docks in Guam, and a horse-drawn hearse said to tailgate midnight travelers on country roads in England, and . . . well, plenty of other stuff,

---

1. Around our house we call this *getting Borleyfied,* a term coined after a night spent learning way too much about the Borley Rectory. Despite the availability of plenty of online debunking, every one of those stories seemed real enough that night.

including one story that had my dad loading us into our '66 Dodge for a drive up to the Napa Valley, where we parked in the old Yountville cemetery and spent a long night looking for ghosts.

For most everyone who writes horror, nights like those were when the hook was set. Well, maybe not so much the "looking for ghosts" part, but definitely the stories. That's what I was thinking about when I sat down to write *Dark Harvest.* Campfire stories, not-so-urban legends, and the particular power they hold. That was the kind of story I wanted to tell. Writing the first section of *DH,* I imagined myself whispering the opening sentences through the rising smoke of a campfire, then reaching through the flames to pull the listener into that strange little town.

In short, I was after fictive immersion in a seriously undeniable way . . . and a particular brand of immediacy, too.

Studied reader reactions? Nope. Wasn't interested in that.

Reactions from the gut and heart? Yes. Definitely.

Most of all I wanted a voice that would carry my story through those cornfields and down the black road, hopefully pushing it across the finish line without giving readers a chance to catch their collective breath. It seemed that voice was the secret, and I worked on it more than anything. Early on I kept trying to wedge more dialogue into the book until I realized *Hey, Norm, the whole book is dialogue!* Maybe that's why I read *DH* aloud during the editing process more than any other story I've worked on. I wanted the words to have a certain rhythm and cadence, and I wanted the voice to fall somewhere between the one I remembered from my dad's stories and my own voice. And maybe that's why folks who know me as a friend rather than a writer often say: *Norm, when I read* Dark Harvest *I could hear you in my head.*

As reviews go, that sets the bar in a place I really like.

There are other things I could say about *Dark Harvest,* and the particular kind of logic I injected into the story, but I don't want to write a book report on my own novel. Other folks can do that. Instead, I'd rather just thank you for giving *DH* a read. I never take that for granted, and I hope the story stirred some of the same things in you that it stirred in me while writing it.

But before I leave you, I'd be remiss if I didn't say a word about Ed Gorman, the writer to whom *Dark Harvest* is dedicated. Early on, Ed bought several of my stories for a string of theme anthologies he edited with Marty Greenberg. He became a mentor and friend, encouraging me to push ahead writing stories that fell somewhere between horror, crime, and noir, tales that didn't necessarily follow the horror template back in the day. Not everyone was giving me that kind of advice. In fact, some folks were doing the opposite of that. Then one afternoon on the phone, during a conversation about writing-to-market, Ed summed it all up and gave me one of the best pieces of writing advice I've ever gotten. "Norm," he said, "you can't fake a worldview."

I've never forgotten those words. It's such simple advice, really. But I've come to realize it's also what writing fiction boils down to: honesty. With the stories you tell, and the places you write about, and the people (and monsters) who populate them.

Thanks, Ed.

And thanks to all of you for hanging out while the coals burn low.

Until next time. . . .

Norman Partridge
Northern California
March 17, 2022

About the Author

NORMAN PARTRIDGE is the author of six novels and six short story collections. His fiction—including *Dark Harvest,* which is being adapted into a film by MGM—ranges from horror and crime to the fantastic. He lives and writes in California.